P9-DUD-606

BILLY SURE

KID ENTREPRENEUR

AND THE HAYWIRE HOVERCRAFT

INVENTED BY **LUKE SHARPE**
DRAWINGS BY **GRAHAM ROSS**

SURE HOVERCRAFT

Simon Spotlight

New York   London   Toronto   Sydney   New Delhi

This book is a work of fiction. Any references to historical events, real people, or real places are used fictitiously. Other names, characters, places, and events are products of the author's imagination, and any resemblance to actual events or places or persons, living or dead, is entirely coincidental.

SIMON SPOTLIGHT
An imprint of Simon & Schuster Children's Publishing Division
1230 Avenue of the Americas, New York, New York 10020
This Simon Spotlight edition May 2016
Copyright © 2016 by Simon & Schuster, Inc. Text by Michael Teitelbaum.
Illustrations by Graham Ross. All rights reserved, including the right of reproduction in whole or in part in any form.
SIMON SPOTLIGHT and colophon are registered trademarks of
Simon & Schuster, Inc.
For information about special discounts for bulk purchases,
please contact Simon & Schuster Special Sales at 1-866-506-1949 or
business@simonandschuster.com.
Designed by Jay Colvin
The text of this book was set in Minya Nouvelle.
Manufactured in the United States of America 0416 FFG
10 9 8 7 6 5 4 3 2 1
ISBN 978-1-4814-6195-5 (hc)
ISBN 978-1-4814-6193-1 (pbk)
ISBN 978-1-4814-6194-8 (eBook)
Library of Congress Catalog Card Number 2015950425

Chapter One

Home again

I'M BILLY SURE—PIZZA LOVER, DOG OWNER, aND kid inventor. I do a lot of different things, including talking to my mom over video chat. Why do I talk to her over video chat? Because my mom has a super-confidential, TOP-SECRET secret—she's a spy, and she's always off doing spy things!

Yup, that's right, my mom is a spy, complete with coded messages, hidden documents, secret missions . . . you know, all the cool spy stuff.

So sometimes, when she's away on secret

missions, the only way I can talk to her is over video chat. Like now.

"I miss you, Billy," Mom says from my laptop screen. "I can't believe it's been two weeks!"

"Me too," I say. "Wow. Two weeks already!"

Okay, so backstory. I didn't *always* know my mom is a spy. In fact, I only just found out a few weeks ago. Mom used to claim she was a scientist doing research for the government. I thought this was true until my thirteenth birthday, when she surprised me by sharing her *real* profession. And then she surprised me even more by taking me to her agency's Spy Academy, where I took spy classes and built inventions to save secret agents on dangerous missions.

This is all 100 percent real. Mom was so impressed with all the inventions my company, **SURE THINGS, INC.**, has produced—inventions like the ALL BALL, which turns into any sports ball; the SIBLING SILENCER, which, uh, silences your siblings; and the STINK

SPECTACULAR, which smells super gross but tastes super great. We're also the company that created GROSS-TO-GOOD POWDER, which makes gross food taste delicious. (If you eat in my school cafeteria, you're welcome!) Our latest invention is the NO-TROUBLE BUBBLE, an impenetrable bubble where nothing can get to you. (Not even those silenced siblings!)

But it's been a while since Sure Things, Inc. has come out with a new product, what with my being away inventing at Spy Academy. That was a lot of fun, but I realized that I'm not cut out to be a full-fledged secret agent. I also missed my best friend and Sure Things, Inc.'s CFO, Manny Reyes. So I decided to come home, even if it meant going back to boring "normal" school and dealing with Emily, my boring "normal" older sister.

Like Mom said, it's been two weeks since I got home from Spy Academy, and this video chat is the first time I get to catch up with her. Seeing her face is really nice. I can almost forget that she isn't safe and sound at home, rather than possibly battling **DANGEROUS NUNCHUK-WIELDING NINJAS** in—well, who knows where the lair of dangerous nunchuk-wielding Ninjas is!

"It feels like I was just at Spy Academy," I tell Mom, "although I've been pretty busy. That's because I told everyone I was on vacation in Barbados, and I had to do a whole report on my trip to Barbados in social studies class. Thankfully, Manny helped me with that research."

Mom laughs.

"Sorry about the extra assignment. Has the rest of school been all right?" she asks.

"It's been okay. When I was away, the Fillmore Middle School Inventors Club elected a temporary president. Do you remember Clayton Harris?"

"Of course!" Mom says. "He was, um—"

"Not super cool, yeah," I say. "The one whose favorite activity is going to the dentist. Well, he was elected club president, and I decided to let him keep that position. I still want to help the club, but I don't have time to run the day-to-day details anymore. Besides, Clayton has done really well as the president. He's found his place. He's made new friends, he's a good leader of the club, and he's even become kind of popular—or at least less *un*popular."

Mom smiles widely. "That is WONDER-FUL!" she says. "Who knows, maybe Clayton will be president of the country someday, all thanks to your club!"

I try to imagine Clayton running for president or nestled into Mount Rushmore or kissing babies, but all I can picture is the same kid who blew chocolate milk out of his nose at my birthday party.

this is chocolate milk

"And how are things at Sure Things, Inc.? Is Emily still helping out?" Mom asks.

"Sure Things, Inc. is okay," I say. "Manny and I are working on something *really* big—a hovercraft. And now we're feeling the pressure to get this invention out as our Next Big Thing." Just to fill you in, our hovercraft is going to be the coolest invention ever. It'll really fly and it'll change the face of transportation as we know it. There's just one little problem. We haven't quite figured out how to make it fly. Manny is waiting on some "QUALITY WINGED MATERIALS" to arrive from overseas. I'm not sure exactly what that means, but Manny says they're the latest in hover technology.

"As for Emily, she and Manny got along okay while I was away, but she's been in a pretty grumpy mood ever since I got home."

"What now?" asks Mom. "I talked to her on her birthday a few days ago and she seemed perfectly happy."

Right—Emily's fifteenth birthday. She might

1

have been all smiles on her video chat with Mom, but the day was *anything* but fun for me and Dad.

It started like this: Emily woke up and started whining for Dad to take her to get her learner permit. Honestly, I didn't see why the permit was such a big deal. All it does is allow her to take a driver's test next year when she's sixteen—or to drive with an instructor now. It's not like she can pick up her friends and drive to the mall by herself.

But anyway, Emily kept on complaining.

Dad tried to remind her that it was a weekend, so the drivers office was closed.

"It's not *fair*," she sniffed. "Mom took Billy on a trip for his birthday! No one's offered *me* a trip. *I* want to go somewhere. And I can't even get my stupid learner permit."

"Actually, I was working the whole time I was at Spy Academy," I tried to remind her, but Emily ignored me. Emily usually ignores things I say when they don't support her argument. So she complained ALL DAY until the next morning when Dad took her to the drivers office first thing. *Then* Emily started pestering Dad about when he would take her out to learn to drive.

I tell Mom all of this and watch her expression change to a frown.

"I wish I could be there to teach her how to drive," she says. "I always feel so guilty that work keeps me away from you kids."

"It's okay," I tell her. "Dad will totally teach Emily how to drive, but he's just a little busy right now. His artwork was accepted to an art gallery."

My dad is an artist, and a pretty good one—if you consider close-ups of my dog Philo's toenails "pretty good." He has a studio in the backyard—a converted garden shed, actually, but he likes it. He can spend days at a time out there painting and be perfectly happy. I'll never understand why a gallery is interested in his WACKY PORTRAITS, but I'm proud of him anyway.

I think Mom is thinking the same thing I am because she starts to laugh, which makes me laugh. In a few seconds we're both roaring to the point of tears, imagining Dad at an art gallery showing fancy art-lovers some portraits of Philo's butt!

So Fancy!

"So what's going on over at Spy Academy?" I ask when I stop laughing long enough to catch my breath. "How's Agent Paul?"

Agent Paul is my mom's partner on her spy missions. And oh yeah, he just happens to be an octopus.

"He's doing SWIMMINGLY," Mom replies, chuckling at her own silly joke, one I'm sure she's made a hundred times before.

"But seriously," she continues, "I've been keeping a very close eye on Drew. So far, at least, he seems to be behaving. He even helped us catch another online scam artist."

I frown at the mention of Drew. At Spy Academy I became very close friends with him, but then Manny found out my new friend was actually the nephew of Sure Things, Inc.'s arch nemesis, Alistair Swiped, CEO of Swiped Stuff, Inc. That wouldn't have been a problem, except Drew was trying to sabotage my inventions the whole time! Like uncle, like nephew, I guess. I let Mom know, but she thought it was best for Drew to stay at Spy

Academy. Maybe some of his EVIL GENIUS can be tamed under careful supervision.

Now that I stop to think about it, it really is amazing how much has gone on in the couple of weeks since I got back. Just talking about all of it makes me tired . . . which reminds me that I've got a busy day of school and inventing ahead tomorrow.

"I think I'm going to go to sleep, Mom," I say. "Lots to do tomorrow. We've really got to get this hovercraft out ASAP."

"Okay, honey, get some sleep. I love you."

"I love you too, Mom," I say.

My monitor goes blank.

I'm always a little sad at the end of a video chat with Mom, but somehow, knowing the truth about her makes it all a bit easier. My mom is off saving people. And that's pretty cool.

Chapter Two

attack of the Monstrous Ladybugs!

THE NEXT MORNING I SLIDE INTO MY CHAIR AT THE breakfast table. Emily is already sitting at the table, sulking, her face buried in her phone. Dad stands at the griddle, flipping something round, red, and gooey. No way can those gooey things be pancakes.

"It's a PANCAKE MORNING," Dad announces, sliding a stack off the griddle and onto a big platter. I guess I was wrong. "*Tomato* pancakes to be exact."

Emily groans but doesn't say anything. My dad isn't exactly a world-class chef, but he thinks he is. He's always coming up with crazy meals and making us force them down. He's actually more like a mad scientist of food, and his dishes are his monsters!

I do eat tomatoes in omelets sometimes, so maybe tomatoes in pancakes won't be too bad. Still, I glance over at the Gross-to-Good Powder in the salt shaker on the table, glad that it's always there.

"Pancakes, not waffles, huh?" I say to Dad. "I guess this means that Mom isn't coming home anytime soon."

One of the many things I learned during my time at Spy Academy was that some of Dad's crazy food concoctions are actually SECRET CODED MESSAGES from my mom. Because she's a spy, her e-mails are always in danger of being hacked, so she and Dad worked out a system. For example, waffles mean that Mom will be coming home soon, and different ingredients in the waffles stand for other information. Dad doesn't have to make the dishes, but he usually does anyway. Tomato pancakes mean . . . well, I'm not exactly sure what tomato pancakes mean.

"Nope, your mother is off on assignment," Dad says, confirming what I thought. "I picked pancakes to make, specifically tomato pancakes, because I thought they'd make an excellent subject for my next painting."

"Of course Mom's not coming home," Emily chimes in, finally taking her eyes off of her phone. "Why should she come home? After all, if my fifteenth birthday wasn't important enough to come home for, why should she come home now?"

I want to remind Emily that she and Mom video-chatted on her birthday, but I think better of it. We're probably going to have to hear about how Mom didn't come home for Emily's fifteenth birthday all the way up until she turns sixteen. And worse, she's just getting started.

"Not only didn't I get a visit, but I'm not getting a BIRTHDAY BEACH TRIP," Emily continues as Dad places a stack of tomato pancakes on the table.

I consider bringing up the point once again that *I* didn't exactly get a birthday beach vacation either. And that my "vacation" was working, going to school, and foiling a dastardly plot by an evil genius. But if there's anything I know about my older sister, it's that talking to her when she's GRUMPY leads to bad news. I shove a pancake into my mouth and pretend to concentrate really hard on chewing.

Glug! Uh-oh. I should *not* have crammed the entire pancake into my mouth. Now it's too late to sprinkle Gross-to-Good Powder on it, and let's just say: tomato pancakes? *Not* delicious.

"And to top it all off, *you* won't teach me to drive!" Emily says now, glaring right at Dad.

Poor Dad, I think.

"I never said that I wouldn't teach you," Dad replies, dropping a few more blobs of pancake batter onto the griddle. I think one of them has a tomato stem in it. "I just said that now is not the right time."

And then Emily goes silent. She realizes

that having this conversation for the FIVE-HUNDREDTH time this week is getting her nowhere. She reaches over and grabs a pancake, dropping it onto her plate.

As Emily's hand passes my face, I notice that she is wearing some weird black gloves. This is odd—I mean, who wears gloves to eat breakfast? This is likely Emily's new "thing." Emily always has a thing that she's into for a few weeks, and then it mysteriously disappears. One time it was wearing glasses with no lenses in them. Another time it was speaking only in a British accent.

Speaking of speaking, we eat the rest of breakfast in silence. I'm thinking about when the winged parts will come in for the hovercraft. Dad is probably thinking about his art gallery. And Emily? Who knows what goes on in her brain.

When I'm done eating, I head out for school.

"Hey, Sure, I still don't see any TAN on you," Peter MacHale says to me as I rush to class.

"Who goes to the beach and doesn't come home with a tan?"

Okay, first of all, that's about the tenth time Peter MacHale has said that to me since I've been back. (Peter is one of those kids who is really chatty in the hallways, but is pretty quiet in class.) Secondly, it's been two weeks since I returned from "the beach," and any tan I might have had would be long gone anyway.

"That because of my newest invention—PERMANENT SUNSCREEN," I reply, forcing a smile. "See ya."

I mean, Permanent Sunscreen isn't a terrible idea. It's just not the Next Big Thing.

After school I pick up Philo and head over to the World Headquarters of Sure Things, Inc., which is very conveniently located in Manny's garage.

Even though I've been back at work for a few weeks, I still get a thrill at the sight of my own workspace. Everything about the Sure Things, Inc. office is perfect. *Especially* our pizza

18

machine, which makes pizza with any toppings you want! I help myself to a slice with pepperoni and peanut butter, which actually tastes really good.

But of course, working at the office isn't just eating pizza with your best friend. It's also about business. Which means working on the hovercraft.

Right now, the hovercraft is just a hulking work-in-progress mess in the middle of the room. I can't really do much until we get the parts in.

I look over at Manny. He's staring at his laptop screen, rubbing his forehead.

"Hey, Manny, how's it going?" I ask. Manny's been in such a good mood since my return, I hate to push him on stuff.

Still, Manny would be the first one to say "business is business," and the business of the moment is getting this hovercraft to fly.

"Hmmm," Manny mumbles in reply—a typical signal that he is deep in thought.

He turns to me. "I'm stuck. Here's what I've

come up with: THE HAPPY HOVERCRAFT? Or THE HOVER PAL? Or maybe THE FLYING FRIEND? Weak, right?"

That's my partner, obsessing over choosing the right name for an invention that I haven't even invented yet. Although it can a bit frustrating at times, Manny's laser focus on the marketing end of things is reason #612 why I'm glad he's my business partner.

"They're all terrible, right?" Manny asks. "You can tell me."

I agree that they are terrible names, but I would never just come right out and say that to him.

"Manny, let's just focus on the hovercraft itself for now," I suggest.

"Hmm . . . maybe you're right, Billy," he says. "I've just never been this stumped before on a name."

I decide that this is not the best time to bring up the fact that Manny's original suggestion for the name of the All Ball was the "Ball Ball Ball Ball Ball." Yup, five balls—like the five balls each model of the All Ball turns into. Somehow I don't think that product would have been as successful.

Right then there's a knock at the door. Manny heads off to get it and comes back with a package.

"Look what just came in!" Manny hollers, holding up a box. "It's the parts we ordered!"

Yes! Finally! The hovercraft prototype looks a little sad without any parts to help fly it. I could probably use some materials we already have, but Manny was adamant on ordering these quality winged materials. Maybe we can finally get somewhere!

Zip! We open the box together. Manny removes the packaging tape neatly. And, oh no . . .

The parts we ordered aren't in this box.

Instead, there are *hundreds* of ladybugs in the box!

"What are we going to do with all of these—" but before Manny can finish, the ladybugs zoom out and fly all around the office!

"Quick! Get the doors!" I shout, and soon we're opening all the windows.

"Shoo! Shoo!" Manny yells at a cluster of the ladybugs. Some of them *zoom* out the window . . .

And some of them land on Philo's nose.

Which is how I learn that Philo really, really doesn't like ladybugs.

"A-rooo! A-woof! A-woooooof!" Philo howls. He stomps around, trying to scare the ladybugs away, and rams buttfirst into my prototype!

"Philo!" I call out, but it's too late. The prototype crashes into many pieces . . . and now it's got a sizeable print of a dog butt.

Maybe I should donate this to Dad's art gallery. . . .

"I think they sent us the wrong package," Manny says quietly. At this point we've gotten most of the ladybugs out—although a straggler lands on my arm and I flick it off.

"You ordered *winged* parts, right?" I ask.

Manny nods.

"Well, they certainly sent us a lot of wings," I say. "Maybe they didn't get the order wrong after all."

After swatting another set of ladybugs away from my slice of pizza, I take a bite and sigh. It doesn't look like we're getting any flying parts soon, and now I have to make a whole new prototype, since Philo wrecked the old one.

"I think it's time to try building the

hovercraft with materials we already have," Manny suggests, looking at some of the parts around the office—which include things like an old skateboard, tons of wires, and a random rainbow wig.

There's a reason why Manny and I are under a lot of pressure for this invention. First of all, Drew Swiped tried to steal the idea when I was at Spy Academy. Second, Sure Things, Inc. hasn't released anything since the No-Trouble Bubble, and even then, it was a joint partnership with our Next Big Thing contest winner, Greg.

"GREG!"

I accidentally shout his name.

"Greg?" Manny asks.

"Remember? The No-Trouble Bubble was supposed to have a hover feature in it, but when that didn't work out, we decided to call Greg when we *do* work on a hovercraft."

The answer seems so obvious, I can't believe I hadn't thought of it before.

Manny smiles. "You're exactly right! We need to talk to Greg right away!"

With that, Manny turns back to his computer to shoot off an e-mail to Greg. I get back to work, re-creating the "craft" part of the hovercraft that Philo destroyed. Thankfully it doesn't take too long to re-create—after all, it still doesn't fly.

When it gets late, I head home. I'm almost out the door when I hear Manny's voice:

"THE HOVER-MATIC?"

"Good night, Manny," I say, hopping on my bike.

At home I head upstairs to my room, ready for an evening of homework. I pass Emily's open door. She's still wearing the black gloves she had on at breakfast, typing away on her tablet.

"Gotten the hovercraft to fly yet?" she asks, showing the most interest in my work since I came home.

"No, but we've decided to ask Greg to come in and help us," I reply.

Emily stops typing and shoots me a look that can only be described as intense. So intense that I'm suddenly glad my sister isn't a superhero (or supervillain). If she was, she could probably shoot lasers out of her eyes.

"You're asking some STRANGER to help you, but you didn't even think of asking *me*, your inventor-in-chief?" she yelps.

Then, without waiting for an answer, she gets up and **BAM!!!** slams the door in my face.

Emily is right. I didn't even think of asking her. But with as unpleasant as she's been lately, that's no shocker. If she hadn't slammed the door, I would have pointed out that Greg isn't a stranger, he's a business partner. After all, we did work on the No-Trouble Bubble together, and we did release it at as a Sure Things, Inc. product.

But I don't have time to worry about my sister. I have to worry about the hovercraft.

Chapter Three

Helping Hands

THE NEXT DAY AFTER SCHOOL WHEN I ARRIVE AT THE World Headquarters of Sure Things, Inc., Greg is already there. He and Manny are leaning over the new prototype.

"Hey, Greg, thanks for agreeing to help us out," I say.

"Wow, Billy! Great to see you again!" Greg says, shaking my hand enthusiastically.

I like Greg, but it's kind of weird the way he acts as if I'm a CELEBRITY. I'm not really a celebrity. Sure, I've been on a few magazine covers and television shows, but if I were really a celebrity,

I'd be friends with people like the actress Gemma Weston (or at least, I *hope* I'd be friends with her).

"So what's going on with this thing?" Greg asks.

"We're having trouble figuring out how to make this fly," I say.

I reach into the cockpit and crank a handle, spinning it around and around. I start to laugh, recalling old silent movies I've seen of the very first cars ever made that started with someone spinning a crank . . . like this.

The prototype starts to HUM and SHAKE. **Zzzzpt!!!** Sparks shoot out of the dashboard.

"Does it do this every time?" Greg asks.

"So far."

"Hmm," Greg says thoughtfully. "Let me see what I can do."

I always appreciate a fresh set of eyes on a project. Greg flips open the toolbox he brought and pulls out a few tools. Leaning into the cockpit, he takes off the lower panel and starts to tinker around with the wires and connections.

After a few minutes Greg slides back out.

"I think I may have figured something out," he says. "Why don't you fire it up again?"

I climb back into the cockpit and crank the starting handle. The hovercraft is pretty small—it's about the size of a bike, but we can work on making it bigger later. This time even more sparks shoot out. Smoke billows, filling the room.

And then, to my surprise—the prototype lifts off the ground!!!

"It's working!" I shout.

Then the whole hovercraft flips upside down, dumping me onto the floor.

I look up to see to the lopsided hovercraft spinning in a circle, spewing sparks and smoke. Uh-oh.

"DUCK!" yells Manny, somehow anticipating what comes next.

Ka-POW!

The prototype explodes, spewing its pieces all around the office.

Philo dashes from his doggy bed and hides under my workbench.

Manny hits the floor as an electric fan flies past his head.

Greg dives out the back door to avoid a spinning snow tire.

I look up as the smoking ruins of our hard work—yet again—is destroyed.

"I hate to say it, but I think we might need a new design for the main body of the prototype," Greg says.

I think he wins the prize for UNDER-STATEMENT OF THE YEAR. And I thought Manny was good at that.

"I agree," I say, standing. The three of us clean the place up and then get back to work.

This time I decide to use different materials entirely, and end up welding a metal trash can and some other special items together. When it's done, I can't help but think how DIFFER-ENT this prototype looks from the previous ones.

"Time to test it," says Greg.

"I'll take the first test ride," I say, feeling brave, but still putting on my helmet and elbow and knee pads. The first rule of inventing? Safety first.

I slip into the garbage-can cockpit.

"Here goes," I say, then I pull back on the bowling pin lever inside.

The hovercraft **clangs!** and **bangs!** until it starts to lift off the floor!

"It's working!" I cry.

Philo slowly ventures out from under my workbench, curious about the contraption.

When I'm about a foot off the ground, I push the bowling pin forward. It's kind of like the joystick on a video game. The hovercraft starts to fly forward, but then when I go left—**Zip!**—it veers off sharply to the right.

Thankfully I'm only a foot off the ground, but when the hovercraft swings around I realize that I'm headed straight for Manny and Greg.

"I CAN'T STEER IT!" I shout.

Manny and Greg dive for cover as I make another circle around the office. I switch off the machine in a panic, and the hovercraft finally **plops!** down onto the floor, shutting off with a dull thud and a hiss of steam.

"Well, this prototype hovers," says Manny, ever the optimist.

My arm is a little sore from the fall, but other than that I feel okay. I climb out of the cockpit and stand beside Manny and Greg, wondering what to do next. Then it hits me.

"Why don't I bring this problem to the Fillmore Middle School inventors club?" I suggest. The first meeting since I've been back from Spy Academy is actually tomorrow afternoon. "Let's see if anyone there might be able to help us."

"They've been helpful in the past," Manny points out. "Why not?"

The next afternoon Manny's dad helps me take the hovercraft to school in his SUV. Once I'm there, I drag the hovercraft up the front stairs and push it down the hall to the lab where the inventors club is meeting.

I stumble backward through the door, dragging the prototype into the lab.

As I catch my breath and turn around, the entire club bursts into applause.

"IT'S BILLY!" shouts Clayton. He is standing at the front of the lab holding a bubbling concoction in a large beaker. White foam pours over the top of it as the liquid inside changes color from purple to green to orange.

"Welcome home, Billy!" yells out a boy in the front row. "How was Barbados?"

This again.

"Um, fun. Wet. Sandy," I say, immediately thinking how dumb that sounds. I quickly change the subject. "So, what are you working on, Clayton?"

"I call this RAINBOW FIZZ," Clayton explains. "The most thirst-quenching beverage ever invented. Take a sip."

I eye the beaker warily. "Don't worry," Clayton assures me. "I've tested it. All the ingredients are edible."

I am actually pretty thirsty, so I take the beaker from Clayton and sip the bubbling concoction.

"Wow," I say. "I was very thirsty, but just one sip took care of that."

Behind me I start to hear some giggles, and that's when I notice that my arms are now covered with RAINBOW-COLORED STRIPES! "Uh, Clayton?"

"Yeah, sorry about that, Billy," he says.

34

"There are still a few bugs to work out. So, what did you bring us today?"

I quickly fill the class in on the trouble I've been having with the hovercraft prototype.

"I have an idea," says a voice from the back of the room.

It's SAMANTHA JENKINS, who joined the inventors club back when I started it. She is kind of a fan of mine. When she first joined the club, she wrote a poem about me and wanted me to sign her Billy Sure T-shirt. I never thought she was actually interested in inventing. Needless to say, I'm surprised.

"Please come up the front of the room, Samantha, and share your idea," Clayton says.

Mom is right. I'm happy to see how well Clayton, a very shy kid without many friends, has taken to his role as club president.

Samantha walks to the front of the room. She stands there, smiling and staring into my eyes.

"Um, what's your idea, Samantha?" I ask, feeling a little creeped out by her stare.

She peers into the cockpit.

"You have a bunch of engines, I see, but it looks like they are working independently," Samantha says. "I think you should connect all the engines together."

"I invented ELECTRIFIED BUNGEE CORDS," says a boy named Eddie sitting in the front row. "I think they might just do the trick."

"Come on up, Eddie," I say. "Sounds like Samantha's idea is worth a try."

Eddie, Samantha, and I connect the hovercraft's engines with the electrified bungee cords. A few minutes later, it's ready for another test flight!

I climb into the cockpit and start it up. It sounds better already, and there is practically no smoke. I feel optimistic about this working!

Then, **whoosh!** I'm flying—way higher than the last time. This is great!

I try to ease the hovercraft to the left, and that's when I realize that the other BIG PROBLEM has not been fixed. No matter how hard

I try to steer to the *left*, the hovercraft continues to fly to the *right*, circling around and around the room.

And that's when a metal bolt suddenly flies out of the cockpit. It zooms right toward Eddie's head!

He ducks, and the metal bolt lands in a bowl full of a green, globby liquid—which is an invention by a girl named Amber, which is supposed to light up a house at night without any electricity.

The crash sends bits of the globby green stuff into the air, splashing it against a tall metal antenna attached to an experiment by a boy named Philippe, which is supposed to pick up your mother's voice, however far away she may be.

The goopy green globs blaze to life, then explode like fireworks, sending Philippe, Amber, and everyone near them scrambling under their desks.

As for me, the hovercraft starts to tilt, rotating, so that the cockpit opening is now closer to the bottom than the top! I have to hang onto the garbage can section for dear life to keep from falling out.

Slowly, I manage to land the thing—this time in one piece—and climb out.

"Thank you all for your help, but it's time for me to go. My ride home—not the hovercraft—is here," I say to the class as Clayton helps me drag the prototype back through the door. "Despite everything, I'm going to call the hovercraft flying higher a SUCCESS. Keep up the good work, Clayton."

"You too, Billy," Clayton says smiling.

As I haul the prototype back into Mr. Reyes's SUV, I notice that my arms are still striped with rainbow colors.

Chapter Four

Hovercraft at Home

"HOW'D IT GO?" GREG asks ENTHUSIASTICALLY, as I drag the hovercraft back inside the World Headquarters of Sure Things, Inc.

"Better," I report. "The kids in the inventors club actually had some really good ideas, and I did get the thing up to the ceiling. It can probably go up higher, but I didn't test that."

"So we're good to go?" Manny asks. "Because I think I might have the name—THE HOVERBABY!"

Greg and I look at each other. Neither one of us wants to hurt Manny's feelings, but the Hoverbaby? I don't know.

"No, it's not working perfectly yet," I say, trying not to give my opinion on the name. "It's still flying a little to the right. Definitely not safe for long flights."

"So, what do we do now?" Greg asks.

Manny and I look at each other. We've been here before, and we both know what needs to be done.

"Sleep-invent," we say together.

"If all goes well, I should have working blueprints for us tomorrow," I say. Usually, when I'm REALLY CLOSE to finishing an invention, I go to sleep and my brain creates the finished blueprints for me.

Having decided this, Manny heads over to his computer. "Check this out," he says.

Greg and I lean over Manny's shoulder and see a graph charting the rising sales of the No-Trouble Bubble.

"WOW!" cries Greg. "This is amazing! You guys rule!"

I smile, realizing that this is Greg's first experience with a successful invention. I remember how good I felt when the All Ball first took off.

I stare at the hovercraft prototype.

"I think I'll take the prototype home tonight," I say. "It might inspire sleep-me."

"Sounds good to me. Let me give you hand carrying it home," says Greg.

Greg helps me drag the hovercraft through the front door and upstairs into my room. I can't exactly explain why, but I have the strong feeling that having it there will inspire my SLEEP-INVENTING.

Once I have the prototype in my room and Greg goes home, Emily walks over.

"I heard you dragging something into the house and I had to see what it was," she says. "Are you into modern sculpture these days? Trying to give Dad a run for his money as an artist? Or have you decided to give up inventing and become a JUNK COLLECTOR?"

"It's just the hovercraft prototype," I reply.

Her eyes open wide. "Does it really work?"

She moves in for a closer look, reaching into the cockpit and moving the bowling pin around. That's when I see that she is still wearing her black gloves.

"Yeah, sure," I reply. I don't bother telling Emily that I still need to work out some bugs, and she doesn't pick up on the hesitation in my voice.

"Hmm," she says, and without another word walks back to her room.

I do homework for a while, taking my mind off of the hovercraft, and then it's time for dinner.

Dad has made cherry and kiwi lasagna. This meal is definitely going to require some Gross-to-Good Powder.

The mood at the dinner table is quiet and tense. I figure I'll break the uncomfortable silence.

"How are the paintings for your art gallery show going?" I ask Dad.

"FANTASTIC!" he replies between bites of the reddish-green lasagna. "I had this stroke of creativity last night, and now I've got a whole series on cooking ingredients that rhyme. Tomato-potato, zucchini-linguini, beans-greens, you know, like that."

"Cool," I say.

Emily doesn't even look up from her plate. I guess she's still mad at me for not asking her to help develop the hovercraft, and mad at Dad for not teaching her to drive, and mad at Mom for not taking her on vacation. I wonder if she has an app on her phone to keep track of who she is mad at and why.

"Thanks for dinner, Dad," I say, bringing my plate to the sink. "I've got to finish some homework. Nice talking with you, Em."

Okay, I couldn't resist. I thought that little jab might break her out of her silence. No such luck. She doesn't take the bait. She just glares at me and sticks out her tongue.

Who's the more mature sibling here?

Back in my room, I continue doing my geometry homework, but I can't help seeing the prototype out of the corner of my eye. I feel like it's calling to me, taunting me, saying, "BIIIIIIIILLY! COME GET ME TO WORK!" I go to the drawer where I keep sheets and blankets and grab a big white sheet, which I toss over the hovercraft.

There, that's better. *Not* thinking about an inventing problem in the hours before going to sleep usually helps me sleep-invent.

I finish my homework, shoot off a quick e-mail to Mom, and then get ready for bed. As I slip under my covers, I hear shouting coming from downstairs.

"I studied really hard to get my learner permit!" Emily shouts.

"I know, honey, and I'm proud of you," says Dad in a calm voice.

"I even bought these special driving gloves!" Emily yells.

So that's what those black gloves are, I think.

"It's not fair! Why won't you teach me to drive?"

"Of course I'll teach you to drive, honey," says Dad. "But it's going to have to wait a couple of weeks. I really have to work on portraits by the gallery deadline next Friday. After that is done, we can start your driving lessons."

I really hate it when my family members argue with each other. Dad sounds reasonable to me. I think Emily is being really impatient and unfair.

A few minutes later I hear Emily stomp up the stairs and **slam!!!** the door to her room.

Eventually, when everything has quieted down, I fall asleep.

I dream that I build a perfect working hovercraft. I hop in, anxious to go for a test ride. But just as I'm about to turn it on, the hovercraft shakes and starts to CHANGE! It morphs quickly into a GIANT BLOB OF JIGGLING JELLY, which wraps itself around me, trapping me inside—and then it launches straight up, through the ceiling, through the roof, and up into orbit around Earth!

OH NO! Trapped inside a jiggling jelly blob!

LICK! LICK! LICK! I wake up for real by way of Philo licking my nose, or as I like to call it, my alarm clock.

I sit up in bed, looking around, trying to shake off the weird dream I just had.

I glance over at the prototype. It is still in a corner, covered by the sheet. Slipping out of bed, I walk to my desk and discover that I really did sleep-invent fully rendered blueprints for a working hovercraft. I see that I've come up with a few minor changes to the basic design, but nothing that should stump us, once I get this blueprint and the current prototype back to the office.

One thing that does surprise me, though, is that it seems the only way to power the hovercraft is with SOCKS! But not just any socks . . . they have be to REALLY STINKY SOCKS! Thankfully, that shouldn't be a problem. After all, I always turn my socks inside out and wear them for two days. A week's worth of my socks could probably keep this thing flying for a long time.

I hurry to the prototype, anxious to look at the changes I'm going to have to work on at the office today. I pull off the sheet. That's when I stumble back in shock.

THE HOVERCRAFT IS GONE!

In its place is a pile of pillows and towels.

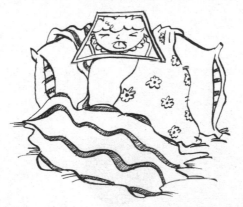

On top of the pile is a picture of Emily sticking out her tongue, and a typed note that reads:

> *Dear Genius,*
> *Since Dad won't let me drive and Mom*
> *won't take me on a trip, I'm going to do both*
> *by myself—in your hovercraft! Sorry I had to*
> *borrow it. I'll return it when I come back—if I*
> *ever decide to come back!*
>
> *In other words,*
>
> *Bye forever,*
> *Emily*

Emily is gone—and so is the hovercraft.

Chapter Five

Emily—Vanished!

PANIC. PANIC. PANIC. PANIC.

Not only has Emily stolen my invention—which is a whole new level of bad just by itself—but she has no idea that the prototype she is flying isn't ready. I could kick myself. I told her last night that it was working!

Which means Emily doesn't know that she can't steer it properly, or that the prototype will take her wherever *it* wants to go, not where *she* wants to go. . . .

Okay, I HAVE TO DO SOMETHING.

But what? What should I do?

Dad. Dad will know!

I race out to Dad's art studio. He's got to be there, right? I mean other than making meals for us, he's hardly left home lately. He'll be there, I'm sure, working on a painting for his gallery exhibit.

I race to his studio. He's not there.

How can he not be there? He's always there! What now?! What now?!?!

That's when I see a note:

> Hi kids,
>
> If you are looking for me I had to go to meet with the gallery director to nail down the final number of Philo's earlobe paintings we should include in my show. Ah, the life of an artist. Be back soon.
>
> Love,
> Dad

I call Dad on his cell and leave a message telling him to call me back as soon as possible. Now what? After another moment of panic, I think of the answer. I'll do what I always do when I don't know what to do . . . talk to MANNY!

I send Manny a quick text to tell him I'm coming over, then I get dressed, snatch up my blueprints, and race downstairs.

I gotta hurry. Emily could be anywhere by now. She could be circling around the neighborhood, or she could be all the way on the other side of the world!

With Philo at my side, I bike at TOP SPEED over to the office. I've got be in school in less than an hour, but I can't even think about that right now. I can't even imagine attempting to concentrate on anything in school until I find out where Emily is. This is a family emergency, plain and simple. I'm sure even Principal Gilamon would understand.

Arriving at the office, I skid to a stop, drop my bike, and hurry inside. Philo follows me, but instead of going right to his doggy bed, which is his usual afternoon routine, he paces back and forth around the office. Maybe being here in the early morning has him confused, or maybe he just senses how freaked out I am.

Have I mentioned that I'm pretty FREAKED OUT?!

Manny is at his computer. I know he usually tries to catch up on e-mail and sales reports before school, so I'm not surprised to find him here. He, however, is surprised to see me, though you'd never know it from his reaction.

"What's going on?" he asks in his usual calm voice.

"Emily!" I shout. "She's gone off on her own trip . . . with the hovercraft prototype."

"Slow down, Billy," Manny says, taking his eyes off his computer screen. "Start at the beginning."

I quickly fill Manny in on what happened.

"Hmm, so Emily is off in a haywire hovercraft," Manny says. "I'll call Greg. I think we

52

need the whole hovercraft team for this one."

A few minutes later, Greg arrives.

"What's that?" asks Greg, pointing to the rolled-up paper under my arm.

"THE BLUEPRINTS," I say. "In all this craziness I completely forgot. I worked out the bugs in the hovercraft last night by sleep-inventing!"

"Let's have a look," says Greg.

I roll out the blueprints and the three of us scan the page.

"So the engines need to alternate in sequence with the electric fans," says Greg.

"Interesting. I don't think any of these changes will be difficult to pull off."

"What's this?" asks Manny, pointing at the design for the hovercraft's fuel chamber.

"That's where you put the really stinky socks," I explain. "That's what fuels the hovercraft. I certainly have plenty of those!"

I check my phone to see if there's a response from Dad yet. No such luck.

"I think we have to build this and go find Emily," Manny says. "It's the fastest way."

Greg and I nod in agreement and we all get to work.

"If you look at this design, the first thing that jumps out is that we need to make this more than a one-person craft," I explain.

Manny, as usual, is one step ahead of me. He drags an old kayak, capable of holding three passengers, into the office.

"I think this will make a pretty good body," he says.

"It's perfect!" I say. "Let's get busy!"

Using the kayak as a body we start to build

out from there. With all three of us working feverishly, the new prototype is soon ready to test.

"I'll take the test flight again," I say, climbing into the roomy cockpit.

I push the starter—an old electric toothbrush—and nothing happens. That's when it hits me.

"There's no fuel in this thing! **GIVE ME YOUR SOCKS**," I say, pulling off my shoes and peeling off my socks. Manny and Greg follow suit. Greg shoves the socks into the fuel chamber.

"This should be enough for a quick test," I say, glancing down at our six bare feet.

This time, when I press the starter, the hovercraft comes to life, humming with a steady rhythm.

I soar up to the ceiling, fly once around the room in one direction, then back around in the opposite direction, feeling in control the entire time.

"**IT WORKS!**" I yelp, and land softly. I'm thrilled that we now have a working

prototype, but I'm still really worried about Emily.

"What are we going to do?" I ask, climbing out of the hovercraft. "I mean we all have to be at school in a few minutes, but we can't just ignore the fact that Emily flew off in an unsafe vehicle!"

"We are going to find her," Manny says incredibly calmly. "After all, what we are doing here, we are doing in the name of science and humanity. Not to mention that this is a FAMILY EMERGENCY."

Manny's deep understanding of the big picture in any situation—life, school, inventing, and Emily's safety—coupled with his always amazing super calmness is reason #224 why I'm so glad he is my best friend.

"I agree," says Greg. "But where do we even start to look for her? She could be anywhere!"

At that moment, Manny gets a **ping!** on his phone indicating that a breaking news story is underway. "Look at this," he says,

opening the story on his phone.
It reads:

Filming for the much-anticipated blockbuster film *Alien Zombie Attack!* is underway at the Really Great Movies studio. Right in the middle of filming a scene in which actress Gemma Weston plays a zombie-fighting secret agent, a REAL spacecraft landed from the sky!

At first the film crew thought it was a new special effect being introduced into the movie, but when it became clear that the cameraman, director, and writer knew nothing about it, panic ensued on set.

No details have yet been released about who—or what—was piloting the spacecraft strangely resembling a trash can. We are left to wonder if this is simply a publicity stunt, or if in fact we are all under attack by a real alien, or zombie, or alien zombie. Are we

doomed? Is this the end of the world as
we know it?

"No!" I scream. "It's not an alien! It's not
a zombie! It's not the end of the world! It's
EMILY in our hovercraft!"

Chapter Six

Team Emily Rescue

"HOW DID EMILY MANAGE TO STEER THE HOVERCRAFT to the movie studio? At least she didn't crash. Still, do you think she's okay?" I blurt out.

"That's the most IMPORTANT THING, of course," says Greg, trying to sound as kind and sympathetic as possible.

"Of course, but there's more to worry about," I explain. "What if word about the hovercraft gets out to the public? I mean, once the movie studio and the press figure out that what really landed was our invention and not a UFO, everyone will know about it! I don't think we're ready for that kind of publicity yet."

Manny remains silent, but I know him well enough to see that he is quietly fuming.

"Why didn't *we* think of that?" he asks.

"Think of what?"

"Of launching the hovercraft with this brilliant publicity stunt!" Manny says. "REALLY GREAT MOVIES should pay *us* for publicizing their upcoming movie! Look at all the press they're getting because of our hovercraft! We missed a major promotion and revenue opportunity here!"

"Um . . . I guess you're right," I say, "but also, what do we do about Emily? I think my mom and dad might be a bit upset if we let Emily fly off in our invention and never see her again . . . even though, according to the note she left, that's what she wants."

Speaking of Dad, I check my phone again. Still no response. He's probably still talking about Philo's earlobes with the gallery director!

"I think we need to finalize a few things on

the hovercraft before we head off on a rescue mission," says Greg, focusing in the thing he came here to do: invent.

"Yeah, the thing flies," he continues, "but it needs a **FEW EXTRAS** before it's ready to go the distance."

Greg pulls out his toolbox and gets to work.

"I'm going to install a high-tech communications device, similar to an old-school walkie-talkie, that's able to cover much farther distances," he says.

Greg leans into the cockpit. He's holding a long black rectangular box with an antenna sticking out and a bunch of knobs lined up.

"Our cell phone signals might get spotty in flight," Greg explains. "This **COMM-DEVICE** will make it easy to communicate with someone on the ground."

Wow! I'm impressed—and a tiny bit jealous—that Greg can invent something this cool, this fast, without even having to sleep-invent.

"Okay, things are looking up. We know where Emily is, and we have a way of getting there," I say. "The movie studio is not that far away. The hovercraft can get us there in no time. But I do think someone should stay here and remain in touch with the hovercraft using Greg's Comm-Device. Just in case there's another Emily sighting or something."

"*Our* Comm-Device," Greg says, correcting me. "We're a team."

I am so glad I chose Greg to help us with this invention. Although if I had asked Emily, we probably wouldn't be in the situation we're in now.

"I'll stay," Greg volunteers.

"I'll go with you, Billy," says Manny. "Should we let your dad know what's going on?"

"ᴅᴀᴅ!" I cry. "He still hasn't called me back. I hope he's out of his meeting."

I snatch up the phone and dial Dad's cell phone number.

One ring.

Two rings. *Come on, Dad. Be there be there, be—*

"Hello?" Dad's voice chimes in my ear.

"Dad!! It's Billy," I say, breathing a sigh of relief.

"Hey, Billy, I'm still in my meeting, but guess what?" says Dad. "The gallery is going to display all seven of my Philo earlobe paintings. ISN'T THAT FANTASTIC?!"

"Yeah, Dad it's great," I say. "But we've got a problem. Emily stole my hovercraft prototype!"

"Well, I'll have to have a word with her," Dad says very seriously. "She knows better than to take something that doesn't belong—"

"That's only half the problem," I say, interrupting him. "She's flown off and has landed at the Really Great Movies studio. I'm at Manny's. We need to go on a rescue mission and save her."

"Give me a couple of minutes to get there," says Dad. "I want to come along and make sure she's okay."

"One more thing, Dad," I say. "Can you stop by the house and raid the hamper for all the REALLY STINKY SOCKS you can find? I'll explain when you get here."

63

I check the hovercraft's settings to be sure we'll be ready to take off as soon as Dad shows.

Which he does, about ten minutes later.

"WHOA!" Dad exclaims. "I thought we were just going to drive, but I guess this, this . . ."

"We built a new hovercraft," I explain. "Way faster than driving."

"All right, I just put the movie studio's location into the hovercraft's GPS," Greg says as Manny, Dad, and I climb on board.

Greg opens up the laundry bag full of really stinky socks that Dad brought from home. He shoves the socks into the hovercraft's fuel tank.

"That's what the socks are for?" Dad asks.

"They're the power source for the hover-craft, Mr. Sure," says Greg.

The engine **hums!** to life and lifts off the floor.

"Let me know if you hear of any more Emily sightings!" I say to Greg, flipping on the Comm-Device and heading to the door.

We fly out of the office and I push the controls harder. The hovercraft climbs higher into the sky. After a few seconds of nervousness about flying so high in a craft that has only had minimal testing, I start to enjoy the thrill of both soaring through the sky and of a successful invention. This thing works PERFECTLY. I have nothing to worry about!

Then it hits me.

"We have to turn around!" I cry.

"What's the matter?" Dad asks. "Is something wrong with the hovercraft?"

"No, the hovercraft is fine," I reply. "It's just that I forgot to show Greg where Philo's food, bones, and toys are. I just left Philo sleeping in his doggy bed."

Ruffff! A surprising but familiar sound comes from just below me. I glance over the edge of the hovercraft's cockpit. There is Philo, hanging from the bottom of the hovercraft by a single paw!

"Philo! He must have jumped onto the craft as we took off!" I reach down and pull Philo into the cockpit.

I give Philo a good pat and he licks my face. Then he puts his front paws up on the edge of the cockpit, allowing the wind to press back his ears.

"Should we turn around and bring him back?" I ask.

"No time," Dad replies. "We've got to make sure that Emily is okay. Looks like Philo just became part of TEAM EMILY RESCUE!"

Greg's voice comes crackling through the Comm-Device.

"I added a little something extra for you guys," he says. "Press the red button on the side of the Comm-Device."

I press the button. Music suddenly blares from its speaker.

"I loaded in some of your favorite tunes," says Greg.

"Thanks," I say, cranking up the volume to Dustin Peeler's new hit song. He was off the radar for a while, but after an awesome performance on the TV show *Sing Out and Shout!*, he is back in business.

Manny and I sing and dance around the cockpit. For the first time in as long as I can remember, I feel like a REGULAR KID. I'm not a world-class inventor with a big company, not the (well, former) president of a school club, not a spy tasked with saving the world—I'm just a kid who is hanging out with his best friend, his dad, and his dog in a hovercraft.

I switch on the hovercraft's cruise control and tear into a bag of chocolate chip cookies that Manny had the good sense to bring along. Together we polish off the cookies in no time. But as I turn up the music for the next song, something starts to go HORRIBLY WRONG with the hovercraft!

"We're losing altitude!" I cry, watching as the hovercraft starts slowly slipping downward.

I push the controls as far forward as they will move. We continue to move downward at a turtle's pace. Still, even turtles hit the ground eventually. . . .

"Check the fuel gauge," Dad says calmly.

It's almost on EMPTY!

I grab the Comm-Device. "Greg, we need more really stinky socks!" I yell. "And we need them fast—or this thing is going to crash!"

Chapter Seven

Really Great Movies!

GREG'S VOICE COMES CRACKLING THROUGH THE Comm-Device.

"Got it!" says Greg. "I'm transmitting the GPS coordinates to you now. Over, Billy."

A blinking light appears on the Comm-Device's screen, showing a location not far from where we are. I guide the sinking hover-craft over there ASAP!

As I'm making the soft crash landing, I realize that I have no idea what place Greg is sending us to. I guess it doesn't really matter as long as they sell socks.

THE CRAZY SOCK DEPOT

"There it is!"

Manny, Dad, and I all look down at a huge sign that reads: THE CRAZY SOCK DEPOT.

It looks like Greg found us the perfect place!

"Hang on, everyone!" I shout, bracing myself.

We hit the blacktop of the Crazy Sock

Depot's parking lot and skid toward the enormous building, spinning in a circle. Trees, cars, and people go whizzing by.

After a few seconds, the hovercraft **screeches** to a halt.

I open my eyes and see that we've stopped about two feet from the front door of the store.

"Everyone okay?" I ask.

"Do you think you could have landed a little closer?" Manny says, keeping a perfectly straight face. "I *guess* we could grab a taxi from here."

"Nice flying, Billy," says Dad reassuringly.

Dad has always been a little on the wacky side—like with his art and food creations—but I never expected him to be this . . . well, *cool.* Even in the face of danger, Dad rocks it. I wonder how many times Dad has been on a dangerous mission before—has my mom ever dragged him along to any of her spy assignments?!

I enter the store with Manny, Dad, and Philo close behind me. I'm stunned. Socks. There are socks everywhere. Socks covering the ceiling fans, socks pinned to the salespeople's pockets, socks hanging from the ceiling. It's really the perfect place to refuel a sock-powered hovercraft.

But, true to its name, the Crazy Sock Depot has no NORMAL-LOOKING SOCKS—no white socks, no black socks, no solid-colored socks at all.

What they do have are rainbow-colored socks, socks that grow real hair, socks that turn different colors to match whatever outfit you are wearing, and socks that change color based on your mood. They even have socks that give you the ability to read someone's mind.

This last one I doubt, though I really don't have time to investigate. I rush down the aisle, grabbing socks and shoving them into my shopping basket. Manny and Dad do the same in different aisles.

If we weren't in such a rush, I think I would actually like to try on a few of these socks. The "make you taller" socks intrigue me. So do the socks claiming to give you X-ray vision!

But we have no time. We've got to get to Emily, so we have to grab, buy, and get moving.

I reach the checkout counter at the same time as Manny and Dad. Each of us is carrying an ARMFUL OF SOCKS. Dad even has socks coming out of his ears—for real!

"Check this out," says Manny as he dumps

his pile onto the counter. "Socks that solve math problems for you. Now these we could *really* use!"

"And I could use these," says Dad, also dropping his pile onto the counter. "Photographic socks. They store every image you see while wearing them. Too bad we have to burn these up as fuel. We definitely have to come back here the next time we're not on Team Emily Rescue."

Philo has a pair of bacon-flavored socks in his mouth. I'm not really sure why anyone but a dog would want bacon-flavored socks, but I guess I'm not a sock eater, so I wouldn't know.

A few minutes later the four of us are back outside. We each carry a bulging bag of socks. I yank open the fuel door on the hovercraft and shove our socks into the chamber.

"Okay, HERE WE GO," I say once everyone is inside. I press the starter.

Nothing happens. I press it again. Again, nothing.

And that's when it hits me.

"Well, here's a great big DUH!" I say. "These socks may be CRAZY, but they're not STINKY! The hovercraft only runs on really stinky socks."

"No problemo," says Dad. "We have six potentially stinky feet—ten if you count Philo. So come on, boys, LET'S GET STINKIN'!"

I pull the socks back out of the fuel chamber. We each slip off our shoes and the socks we are wearing and put on a pair from the store.

"Okay," says Dad, "let's run around the parking lot until our feet get stinky!"

As I trot behind Dad and just in front of Manny, I see the socks I have put on change from blue to green to white, matching my pants, shirt, and sneakers in order.

Dad's socks start to glow and flash, swirling in rhythm with every step he takes.

Glancing back over my shoulder, I notice that Manny's socks **roaaaaaaar** like a lion every time he takes a step.

After a few trips around the parking lot, we stop, pull off our socks, and smell them.

"Yup, these are definitely stinky," I say, tossing them to the ground.

"Mine too," says Manny, tossing his.

"Mine three," says Dad, adding his socks to the pile.

Philo yips.

We each grab another pair and take off running, with Philo close behind.

This time Dad wears anti-gravity socks. As he runs, his feet lift about an inch off the ground. It looks like he's running on a cushion of air.

"I may have to get a pair of *these* socks to keep!" he says, his face beaming.

Now, why didn't Manny and I think of inventing that one!?

The anti-gravity socks go into the pile. Dad slips on another pair—socks that sing as you move—and goes back to running. The song is an oldie from when Dad was a teenager, and he happily sings along as he runs. Philo chases, howling a harmony:

Ah-woooooo!

As I watch Dad singing and jogging around the parking lot, I realize how much he is enjoying just being silly, and how much I like hanging out with my dad.

After a few trips around the parking lot, more socks are ready to be added to the stinky pile. We repeat this for a while until the pile is about up to my waist.

"I have an idea," says Dad. "Now that we're all sweating, let's take some more socks and rub them on our armpits. We can get them REALLY stinky that way."

My dad is a genius when it comes to stinky-ness!

"There's no way to know for sure," I say after stink-a-fying some more socks, "but I think we have enough. Let's try it."

Holding my breath, I cram the hefty pile of really stinky socks into the fuel chamber. Then we all climb back into the hovercraft.

I press the starter. It whirrs and buzzes, then the engines roar to life.

"Hang on!" I cry.

"Team Emily Rescue is back in business!" shouts Dad.

We soar back into the sky. I pull on the parachute wings with one hand while adjusting the joystick with the other, setting our course for the Really Great Movies studio.

"THE BIRD IS BACK IN THE AIR," I announce into the Comm-Device.

Greg's voice crackles back out of the speaker. "Good job, guys. I guess those socks did the trick."

"With a little help from us," I explain, pushing the hovercraft to its top speed. I'm in such a good mood about getting back into the air that I have to remind myself that we are still on a serious rescue mission.

We fly into a bank of clouds, making it hard to see where we're going. A couple of minutes later, the clouds break up, revealing a sight that looks as if it's straight out of a dream.

Below us, mountains rise to the sky. MOUNTAINS! There are no mountains where I live. It's as flat as one of Dad's pancakes there. But here there are real, giant, awe-inspiring mountains!

Suddenly one of the mountains ERUPTS! This is not just a mountain, it's a VOLCANO! Flaming orange lava spews from the top and pours down the side of the mountain, sending plumes of thick white smoke right toward us.

"Um, Billy," says Manny, in what passes for panic in my partner.

"On it!" I say, steering us away from the blinding smoke.

As we skirt around the dense white smoke, my view clears again. Looking down I spot a herd of dinosaurs—Brontosauruses to be exact—happily munching tall plants by a stream in a thick jungle.

Um . . . we don't have dinosaurs or jungles where I live either.

"I love dinosaurs!" cries Dad, unfazed by the strange scene below.

Just then, a Tyrannosaurus rex runs into the jungle.

ROOOOaaaaRRRRRR!!!!

Philo jumps up from the floor of the hover-craft, rests his front paws on the edge of the cockpit, and looks down.

ROOOOaaaaRRRRRR!!!!

The T-Rex looks right up at us as he roars again, revealing his long sharp teeth.

YIP! YIP! YIP! Philo barks madly back at the beast.

We pass above the jungle, which comes to a sudden end, giving way to a huge complex of buildings. Below, a crowd of people walks from building to building. But these are not just ordinary people.

A group of hairy beasts and vampires stroll along, chatting as they walk. One holds a computer tablet.

Several zombies, complete with blood dripping from their mouths and hollow, sunken eyes, share sandwiches and sodas, while nearby a pair of three-headed, twelve-armed aliens toss a Frisbee back and forth.

The scenery below changes again, and we fly past the top of a huge spaceship sitting on a launchpad ready to blast off.

In the distance sits a MEDIEVAL CASTLE. A dragon lands on the castle's roof, spreads its enormous leathery wings, and shoots a stream of fire from its mouth.

"I guess we've arrived at the Really Great Movies studio," says Manny. "They specialize in monster, sci-fi, and fantasy movies."

We come to a row of trailers. Actors walk in and out, carrying scripts.

Manny stares intently at the trailers. "Billy, bring the hovercraft down a bit," he says.

When we are low enough, I can read the names on the sides of the trailers.

"Look!" I shout, pointing. "That one says 'Gemma Weston'!"

As I said before, Gemma Weston is one of my favorite actresses. She's about Emily's age and is one of the most popular celebrities in the world. And she's *right here!*

In the midst of this excitement, I almost don't see the name on the next trailer over.

Almost.

Chapter Eight

Emily Sure, Movie Star!

I'M STUNNED.

I'm relieved.

And I'm SUPER annoyed.

I'm stunned to see my sister's name on a movie star trailer—right next to the trailer of my favorite celebrity. This makes no sense in my mind.

I'm relieved, of course, because this means that Emily is safe, that somehow our faulty hovercraft prototype got her here and landed safely.

And, I'm pretty annoyed at Emily for scaring

me this way when she has probably been having the TIME OF HER LIFE!

I guide the hovercraft toward the ground, setting it down gently next to the trailer with Emily's name.

We all climb out. Philo rushes to the trailer.

"Ewwwwww!" comes a bloodcurdling scream from inside.

"Emily!" cries Dad.

Just as Dad takes a step toward the trailer's door to see what Emily is screaming about, the door flies open.

"What is that HORRIBLE SMELL?!" shrieks a voice from the doorway.

The voice sounds like Emily, but what appears next doesn't look like Emily. A zombie stumbles out of the trailer, moaning and walking stiffly right toward me!

I back away, fear and panic shooting through me. Philo whimpers and runs behind my legs. All I can think is that A ZOMBIE HAS EATEN EMILY, and now it's coming for *me*!

And that's when my brain takes a moment

to remember that there are no such things as zombies, and that I am, after all, at a movie studio that makes monster movies.

The zombie stops in front of us, looks up, and breaks into a huge smile.

"Dad! Billy! Manny!" the zombie cries, grabbing the three of us in a group hug. "I'm so glad to see you!"

A clump of zombie flesh lands on my shoulder.

"Emily? Is that you?" asks Dad.

"What? How do you not—oh, the makeup," replies Emily. "Yes, it's me. I've been in this makeup for so long I forgot I was even wearing it."

She sniffs the air. "But what is that smell? It's like, really, *really* dirty laundry, but somehow worse."

"Stinky socks, actually," I explain. "Lots and lots of stinky socks. They're what powers our new hovercraft."

"Well, they smell awful," she says, wrinkling her half-rotted zombie nose. "Still, it *is* nice to know that my gross little brother is useful for something."

Manny, who has been silent since we landed, finally speaks up.

"Am I the only one here wondering what is going on? Emily takes off in a defective, uncontrollable hovercraft, and instead of being in terrible danger, she ends up with her own trailer on the Really Great Movies studio lot, dressed like zombie. Correct me if I'm wrong, but isn't this all just a little bit weird?"

Emily bursts out laughing.

I have to admit, a LAUGHING ZOMBIE is a pretty strange sight.

"First of all, you are all on the set of Really Great Movies' latest blockbuster, *Alien Zombie Attack!* Come in to my trailer and I'll tell you the rest of what happened," Emily says.

Before stepping inside, I ping Greg through the Comm-Device and let him know we're all okay.

We follow Emily inside. I'm amazed at how luxurious the trailer is. Emily must be

A REALLY BIG DEAL. A large flat-screen TV takes up half a wall. A long couch sits along the opposite wall. Philo hops onto the couch and curls right up.

Emily's laptop sits open on a small desk, streaming some music. The trailer also has a full kitchen, complete with a **COTTON CANDY MAKER.** Hmm . . . maybe I'll get one for the Sure Things, Inc. office.

"Who wants a soda or a snack?" Emily asks, pulling open the fridge to reveal that it's fully stocked with delicious-looking stuff.

I grab a soda and half a tuna sandwich. Until this very moment, under all the pressure of our rescue mission, I hadn't realized just how hungry I was. Once everyone is settled comfortably, Emily launches into her story.

"So, as you know, I was pretty upset that everyone has been ignoring me lately—whether it's about driving, or vacation, or

Sure Things, Inc.," Emily starts off.

"I wasn't ignoring you—" I start to say, but Emily cuts me off.

"Sorry, Billy," she says. "But I've got to tell this story now. Anyway . . .

"When Billy brought home the hovercraft, I saw my chance to get out of a house where everyone ignores me. I waited until he fell asleep, dragged the hovercraft outside, and took off. I originally planned on flying to England so I could meet all my favorite British celebrities, but shortly after my flight began I realized that the hovercraft was out of control—"

"A haywire hovercraft," interrupts Manny.

Emily just gives him a look. With her zombie makeup on, I'm a little afraid she might eat his brains, but luckily for Manny she continues with her story.

"So I started losing ALTITUDE and was worried that I might crash. Doing my best to steer the hovercraft, I landed at the nearest open spot—which just happened to be here at the movie studio.

"As soon as I hit the ground a man came running toward me. In one hand he held a computer tablet. In his other hand he clutched an old-fashioned megaphone. He asked me if I was okay, and I told him I was, and then he told me that I was on set for *Alien Zombie Attack!* and introduced himself as Felipe LaVita, the director."

"Felipe LaVita?" Dad interrupts. "But, Emily, he's FAMOUS! He owns this entire movie studio."

Emily smiles. "Yeah, well I know that *now*," she says. "Felipe was so impressed by the hovercraft, he made a deal with me. If I could get the hovercraft to work again, he'd write me into the script—to play Gemma Weston's best-friend-turned-zombie, of course. So I agreed. I mean, I *did* invent Gross-to-Good Powder, so I totally thought I could fix the hovercraft.

"Well, then, get this. Felipe brings out Gemma Weston to meet me! Who just so happens to be my FAVORITE BRITISH CELEBRITY! Gemma and I immediately hit it off, and we bonded over some of the great food she has in her trailer. She's awesome. Anyway, she is one of, like, my best friends now. So we're friends on and off screen." Emily smiles, finishing her story.

"Why didn't you call to tell us you were all right?" I ask. "We were worried."

"Aww, that's so sweet of you, Billy," she says.

She seems to be genuinely touched by my concern, although the expression of sweetness coming from her zombie face—or actually, *any* of Emily's faces—is not very comforting.

"The studio blocks all cell signals during filming," Emily explains. "Felipe is a nut about SECRECY around his films. He's afraid the press will leak spoilers."

"As long as everything's okay, I guess," I say.

"Well, that's the thing," Emily says. "Really Great Movies wants to use the hovercraft in the film. But, despite my best efforts, I can't get it to work again. And so, now that you're here, Felipe, Gemma, and I could really use your help."

Felipe, Gemma, and I? This stardom thing has apparently gone directly to Emily's head!

"So, Billy," she asks. "What do you think? Can you help me?"

Chapter Nine

Philo's Big Adventure

WE FINISH OUR SNACKS AND STEP BACK OUTSIDE. I stand in front of Emily's trailer, thinking about her question. Should I try to repair the first hovercraft prototype so Emily can keep her part in the movie? What about the second version of the hovercraft that brought us here?

And what about having our hovercraft featured in a major movie? Will that be good publicity for the invention and for Sure Things, Inc., or will it be an opportunity for someone—like DREW SWIPED—to steal the idea?

All of these thoughts bouncing around my

mind lead me to just one conclusion. I have to talk this over with Manny.

But before I say a word to Manny or answer Emily, three zombies appear, walking toward us from behind the trailers. This time I'm not startled. After all, I've just spent the last fifteen minutes talking to one.

Philo, however, feels differently.

At the first sight of the walking zombies, Philo freaks out and dashes away.

"PHILO! COME BACK!" I shout, but all I see are his back legs pumping as fast as he can go. "I have to get him!"

I take off, doing my best to keep up with him. No easy task.

Up ahead I see Philo zooming right for the movie set with the spaceship we saw when we first flew over the studio. He jumps over the Do Not Cross tape and lands on the ship!

Nearby, a cameraman points his camera at the spaceship. Standing next to him is another movie director, frantically flipping through the pages of her script.

"A DOG?!" she shouts. "I didn't know there was supposed to be a dog in this movie! I don't see a dog in the script! A dog riding the space-ship? Who changed the story? Why didn't they tell me?! Why doesn't anyone tell me *anything*, I am the *director* of this film—"

"I don't know, Gloria, but the dog looks pretty good up there," says the cameraman.

"He does, now that you mention it," says

the director. "Keep the cameras rolling!"

"That's *my* dog!" I shout.

"Does he have an agent?" the director asks, handing me her business card.

"No!" I shout. "He's not an actor. Look, someone has to get him off that ship. He could get hurt!"

Just then, Philo jumps off the space-ship . . . and lands right on the neck of a FIRE-BREATHING DRAGON!

Philo's eyes open wide in terror as flames shoot from the dragon's mouth.

I spot a crew of technicians that are obviously controlling the mechanical dragon. I hurry over to them.

"You've got to turn the dragon off!" I shout. "That's my dog up on the dragon! You've got to stop the dragon before something bad happens!"

"We're trying!" says one of technicians. She frantically yanks a lever on a control panel. "But the switch is stuck. We can't make the dragon stop breathing fire!"

I look in horror as the dragon's head tilts down, sending flames right into a long rack of costumes that are being transported across the studio lot—aliens, monsters, princesses, and robots—setting the costumes ablaze.

This is not Philo's fault, I think. The dragon is malfunctioning. But I still feel responsible for this GROWING CHAOS. And I'm very worried about Philo's safety!

With fire still spewing from the dragon's mouth, Philo jumps off and lands on one of the heads of a three-headed alien. Philo looks down and finds himself staring into a set of five bulging, floppy eyeballs.

Phew! At least he landed safely without catching on fire or hurting himself.

The alien reaches up, takes Philo off his head, and places him on the ground.

"There's a good doggy," says the alien.

This buys me just enough time to catch up—that is, until the alien goes to pet Philo, who sees a nine-fingered green reptilian hand reaching for him.

Philo panics.

Yip-yip-yip-yip-yip!

He barks, then he takes off, yelping . . . and runs right into a Triceratops who is lumbering along, followed by a cameraman.

"Philo!" I cry out, pushing myself to run faster before Philo scampers away again.

But I'm too late.

Philo is now right between two golf carts. One cart is filled with people being taken to a movie set. The other is filled with hundreds of tennis balls. What is going on at this studio?

"LOOK OUT FOR THAT DOG!" shouts the driver of the cart filled with people, swerving sharply to avoid hitting the other one.

Both drivers slam on their brakes—and the tennis balls come flying out of the back of the second cart, rolling and bouncing in every direction.

Philo runs off.

"I'm really sorry about my dog," I say, walking quickly toward the cart.

As I bend down to pick up some of the tennis balls, I feel my feet going out from under me. I land on the ground on my butt, unhurt, but a bit embarrassed.

"These balls have to be at sound stage nine in five minutes!" says the cart's driver, who jumps out and promptly slips on two tennis balls, also landing on his butt.

I'm torn. I have to rescue Philo before he gets hurt. But I do feel responsible for this mess. The driver and I crawl on the ground, grabbing tennis balls with both hands, tossing them back into the cart.

After a few minutes, all the balls have been picked up.

"Sorry, agai—"

The driver speeds away, mumbling something about "no pets allowed on the lot."

I spot Philo in the distance.

"Philo! Philo!" I shout. But he keeps running. I take off after him.

I'm just about catch up to him when he reaches the base of a mountain. He scrambles up. I start to climb up after him. And that's when the VOLCANO ERUPTS!

Thick red goop spills from the opening at the top of the mountain, sending Philo sliding back down. As he speeds past me, I reach out to grab him, but just miss. Philo ends up at the bottom of the mountain, covered in the red stuff.

He takes off again, leaving red paw prints as he runs.

I finally catch up to Philo at the side of a building. A large door slides open and a Roman-style chariot—filled with gladiators, pulled by a team of horses—comes charging out.

Startled, Philo jumps up and away, and lands right in my arms.

Poor guy. I can feel his heart pounding as I hold him and scratch between his ears.

"It's okay, boy," I say. "You're safe. No more monsters, no more spaceships, no more dinosaurs. Come on, let's clean you up and go see Emily."

I head back to Emily's trailer. On the way, I pass someone watering a big garden with a hose.

"Excuse me," I say. "Could I, um—" I hold up Philo. RED GOOP drips from his fur.

"Sure thing," say the gardener. "I'll set it on gentle spray. You just hold the dog."

A soft shower of water sprays over Philo. He loves it when I spray him with the hose at home, and he now barks happily as the red stuff runs off. The hose stops and Philo shakes the excess water off his fur.

"Thanks so much!" I say, picking up Philo and heading off.

I carry Philo back to Emily's trailer. Standing in front of the trailer, beside Emily, Dad, and Manny, is a tall man in a bright orange shirt and polka-dot pants. And standing next to this man is my favorite movie star in the world . . .

GEMMA WESTON!

Chapter Ten

The Offer

MY MOUTH MOVES. BUT NOTHING COMES OUT. I WANT to say things like, oh, I don't know, "Hello." That would be good for starters. "Nice to meet you." That's a classic. That might work too. But I say nothing.

I'm standing here, STARSTRUCK, my clothes covered in red goop, while at the same time marveling at the fact that I can still feel starstruck. After all, I've been on TV a bunch of times, and I've met celebrities before—I've even shared quite a few stages with Carl Bourette, my favorite baseball player in the world.

But for some reason seeing Gemma Weston, not up on a big screen in a movie theater, but standing here, looking just like, like, well, like just a REGULAR PERSON . . . for some reason, *that* makes me super nervous.

Dad finally breaks the silence.

"Is Philo okay?" he asks.

It's then that I remember I'm still holding Philo in my arms. "Oh yeah. He's fine." I place him on the ground. Philo happily sniffs at Dad, Manny, and Emily, his tail wagging. It's almost like he never went on an adventure to begin with.

Emily speaks up.

"Gemma and Felipe, I'd like you to meet my dad, my brother, Billy, and his business partner, Manny," she says. "Oh, and this is our dog, Philo."

"Nice to meet you all," says Gemma, flashing a smile that could light up a dark room. Then she wrinkles her nose. "Um, I don't mean to be rude, but what is that AWFUL SMELL?"

Manny and I look at each other. I'm face-to-face

with Gemma Weston, and I have to explain to her all about stinky socks.

"Um, well, you see . . ." I stammer. "Well, that is–"

"It's socks," Dad jumps in.

"Excuse me?" says Gemma. "Did you say 'socks'?"

"Actually, only stinky socks work," Dad says, as if it's the most normal thing anyone has ever said.

Gemma squints, tilts her head, and looks over at Emily, clearly hoping for an explanation.

Emily stares at me and raises her decaying zombie eyebrows, from which I gather that Emily doesn't want to explain the whole stinky sock thing to her new pal Gemma.

I'm about to open my mouth, this time to explain to a movie star why she's smelling stinky socks, when Gemma speaks up.

"You know, Billy, you don't have to be embarrassed by having stinky socks," she says. "My socks don't exactly smell like ROSES either."

I smile, immediately at ease.

"Actually they're not all mine," I say. "I need stinky socks from lots of people to power my hovercraft."

Gemma smiles.

Then Felipe LaVita steps forward. I've been so nervous about talking to Gemma, I somehow completely forgot about the man in the colorful outfit.

"I am so filled with happiness to have all of you at the studio right now," he says, shaking hands all around.

"I love all your movies, Felipe," says Dad. "*Monsters from Beyond!, Dinosaurs vs. Dragons!* and my favorite, *Zombies Love to Dance Too, Part Two.*"

Dad does love his cheesy monster movies. One more thing I love about Dad.

"Oh, you are too kind," says Felipe. "But what is the matter? You didn't like *Zombies Love to Dance Too, Part One?*"

Everyone laughs. Dad laughs the loudest.

"But all joking aside, it is so wonderful to meet you all. We love having Emily right here to work on my film," Felipe says. Then he turns and looks right at me.

"So you are the WONDERFUL INVEN-TOR Billy Sure?" Felipe asks.

"Yes, sir," I reply. "And this is my partner at Sure Things, Inc., Manny Reyes."

"Nice to meet you, sir," says Manny.

As always, Manny is polite, but I know my partner well enough to see that he is getting a little impatient with all this chitchat. Now that he knows that Emily is all right, I can tell that he's waiting to see what's next for our hovercraft.

"My heart is singing so loudly I can hardly hear it," says Felipe.

I'm not sure that makes any sense, but I decide not to say anything.

"Sure Things, Inc.! So this is the team behind the No-Trouble Bubble," Felipe continues excitedly. "You know I just used the No-Trouble Bubble in my latest blockbuster, *Bubble Away Your Trouble*. It worked like charms do!"

I glance to my left and see that Manny is gone. I turn around and find him standing by our hovercraft, getting it ready for the trip home.

Felipe looks past me and spots Manny at the hovercraft.

"The HOVERCRAFT!!!" he squeals. "Emily, my darling, you fixed it! You fixed it! It's PERFECT!!! It's perfect for our movie!"

Emily looks a bit embarrassed.

"Actually, Felipe," she says. "That's not the one I landed in. It's a new one that my brother built."

"Of course you built it, Billy Sure!" chirps Felipe. "After all, you invented the No-Trouble Bubble!"

"Well, Mr. LaVita, that was actually my friend Greg's id—"

"And don't forget the Gross-to-Good Powder," Gemma adds, smiling. "I actually used that at a terrible restaurant a few months ago. It really saved me from a potential embarrassing situation with my agent."

"Actually, that one Emily invented," I explain. "I just—"

"Such a talented group . . . so much kindness, too," says Felipe. "And that is why I am going to make you the offer of a lifetime.

"I will give you, Billy, and you, Manny, roles in this movie," he says. "Just like Emily who already is in my movie. She makes such a perfect zombie what with the frowning."

Emily frowns.

Manny looks up from the hovercraft. I can tell he thinks that this is a cool idea. I know *I* do! Though Manny, as usual, controls his excitement—always the cool negotiator. I can see that he is waiting for what is coming next.

Felipe continues.

"*And* I will also put a lot of investment

money into Sure Things, Inc. Does that sound good?"

Now Manny starts to smile. I think it sounds fantastic, though I can tell that Manny is still waiting for the catch.

"So, here is the deal! You two are in the movie, and I invest in your company—in exchange for EXCLUSIVE USE of the hovercraft, here at Really Great Movies studio! Nice, yes, right, yes?"

And that's when Manny's smile disappears. I feel my spirits sink a bit, too. Exclusive rights? I mean, I know I'm not the business expert in this partnership, but somehow that just doesn't sound right. We've never given away the rights to any of our inventions. That would mean we wouldn't own the product anymore, and the products are what make Sure Things, Inc., well, Sure Things, Inc.

What are we gonna do?

Chapter Eleven

a Deal Is a Deal . . . or Is It?

MY GUT REACTION IS THAT THIS IS A BAD IDEA.
Sure it would be great fun to be in a movie, and
getting investment money from Really Great
Movies would definitely take some financial
pressure off of us. But somehow, giving up the
rights to one of our inventions . . . I don't know.

What I *do* know is that the last thing I want
to do is talk about all this in front of Felipe
and Gemma.

"That's a very GENEROUS OFFER, Mr.
LaVita," I finally say.

"No-no-no-please, Billy, you must call me

Felipe like all of my friends like to do. Like darling Emily does. Because I think we are friends, no?"

"Sure, Felipe," I say. "But as far as your offer goes, can Manny and I have a couple of minutes to talk this over?"

"Why certainly, Billy," Felipe says.

Then something else pops into my mind.

"And I think Emily should be part of our conversation, too," I say. "She is a member of the family and a part of the company. This decision affects her as well."

Emily's zombie face lights up. I can tell this is what she wanted all along.

I look over at Dad.

"I've always let you run your business as you see fit, Billy," Dad says. "Whatever decision you make, I support it."

"Here's an idea," Felipe says. "While the three of you talk, why don't I give your dad a quick tour of the studio?"

"Really?" says Dad, his eyes opening wide. "Cool! Thanks!"

"I'll look after Philo, if that's okay," says Gemma. "I love dogs." She scratches Philo's neck, and he does that dog thing where his back leg twitches.

Philo happily follows Gemma into her trailer.

"SEE YA LATER, GATORS!" says Dad as he follows Felipe.

Left alone, Manny, Emily, and I sit down on the steps outside her trailer.

"I don't know about this," I say. "I mean, being in a BLOCKBUSTER MOVIE sounds amazing, and the money would be really helpful for our next Next Big Thing, but something just feels wrong about giving away exclusive rights to something we created."

"Don't forget that Greg was involved in this too," Manny points out. "Actually, now that I think of it, we should give him a call."

Uh-oh. Involving Greg in more Sure Things, Inc. business might not go over so well with Emily. I look at her, but thankfully she's smiling. She doesn't look jealous. Just in case she is, I tell her that she can be the one to call Greg and fill him in, since she's good at telling stories and all. I think she likes the compliment.

"We can't pass this opportunity up!" Greg says after Emily tells him everything.

"I agree," says Manny. "And with the money from the Really Great Movies studio, we could move right into working on our next invention without having to seek out new investors."

"But this could be Sure Things, Inc.'s most successful invention yet!" I point out.

"EXACTLY," says Manny. "And though it sounds weird, this invention could end up being a huge headache for us."

"What do you mean?" I ask, genuinely confused.

"Think about it, Billy," Manny says, "We might have simply invented something *too* good. We were able to get here without a problem, but what if there were *other* hovercrafts in the sky? If we release this so that thousands of people can buy it, we could end up disrupting

air travel. Picture a sky full of hovercrafts above every major city."

I hadn't thought about that. Manny is right. This is not just some invention that people will use in their own spaces. This hovercraft will be a whole new way to travel.

"Think about how fast the general release of the hovercraft would bring on government regulations, air traffic control issues, and on and on," Manny continues. "I say let's take the investment money for Sure Things, Inc.'s NEXT BIG THING."

Emily nods in agreement.

I see their point. I guess it does make sense, even though it still feels a little strange.

A short while later Felipe returns. Dad is still on his tour of the studio, this time speaking with the cameraman over by the fire-breathing dragon.

"So, Billy Sure, have you made a decision?" he asks.

As I open my mouth, Felipe interrupts me.

"Oh, wait! I almost forgot. Before you make

up your minds for the final time, I would like to make the offer a LITTLE SWEETER."

Manny raises an eyebrow. Emily leans in closer, and another glob of fake zombie skin slides off her face. Felipe continues:

"Really Great Movies will not only put you in the movie and invest in the company, but we will also create a hovercraft ride at the Really Great Movies theme park, complete with a sign letting everyone know that this was invented at Sure Things, Inc. And, of course, you both will get lifetime passes to the park. Emily too, naturally."

"And our friend Greg, too?" says Billy. "It was his idea, and he helped us finish the hovercraft."

"Yes, Greg too, of course. Of course!"

Then I remember something else.

"And the members of the Fillmore Middle School inventors club? We got some great ideas from them, too."

Felipe nods. "Of course! Of course!"

This makes sense to me. I love the idea

of people being able to fly the hovercraft at the theme park, rather than out in the world, which, as Manny pointed out, could cause ALL KINDS OF TROUBLE.

"So, do we have a deal?" Felipe asks.

I look over at Manny and Emily. They both nod enthusiastically.

"Yes, Felipe," I reply, extending my hand. "We are having a deal."

"And, I think you just solved the problem of what to call the invention," says Manny.

I had almost forgotten about Manny being stumped on a product name for the first time in his life.

"Since the hovercraft is now the property of Really Great Movies, I think we should call it . . . the REALLY GREAT HOVERCRAFT!"

"I love it!" says Felipe. "A deal is a deal!"

Manny is happy. Everyone loves the name, and we can officially close the books on this invention—something that always makes Manny's day. As an added bonus, Felipe says we also get to ride the hovercraft any time we want—WITHOUT WAITING IN LINE!

Emily is beaming. Not only is she getting a chance to be in a movie and hang out with Gemma Weston, but her wild hovercraft ride has now led to a really great deal for Sure Things, Inc.

"Oh, and one more thing," Emily says.

Uh-oh, I hate it when Emily says "ONE MORE THING." You never know what that one more thing is.

"I know I'm inventor-in-chief and all of Sure Things, Inc., but we all know that's not really a good title for me. If we are working with the Hollywood movie industry now, can I be the the Sure Things, Inc. VERY OFFICIAL HOLLYWOOD COORDINATOR?"

That's it? That's all she wants? I smile.

Manny shrugs. "Why not?" he says.

Emily screeches, "YAAAAAY!" **Plop!** Another piece of zombie flesh falls off her face and squelches on the ground.

"Glad to see everybody is happy!"

I turn around and see Dad, back from his

tour. He looks like a kid who has just gotten home from his favorite theme park, which I guess is what he is right now.

"Look what I got!" he shouts, holding up a rubber monster mask.

Dad pulls the mask over his head. His monster has eyes that have melted halfway down to his cheeks. His mouth is on the side of his head where his ear should be.

"How do I look?" he asks in a voice muffled by the mask.

"Very handsome, Dad," says Emily.

Dad pulls off the mask.

"The tour was so cool! I got to visit the costume and makeup department, and the special effects department. Look what I got there!"

Dad holds up a TOY MODEL of a spaceship. It looks identical to the spaceship that Philo jumped on.

Felipe turns pale and starts waving his arms frantically.

"Uh, no that is not a toy, no-no-no-no," he sputters. "That belongs to the department for special effects. No-no-no, I will take that back, please."

"Oops. Sorry!" says Dad, handing the space-ship back to Felipe.

Felipe composes himself, and then turns back to me, smiling.

"Really Great Movies is PROUD to work with Sure Things, Inc.!" he says.

Chapter Twelve

The Really Great Hovercraft

"I HAVE ONE MORE REQUEST, BILLY," says Felipe. "Could you take me on a test ride?"

"Sure," I say, happy for an opportunity to fly the prototype one last time before handing it over to the studio.

Felipe and I climb into the hovercraft.

"Hang on," I say, "HERE WE GO!"

I press the starter button. Nothing happens. I press it again. Still nothing.

Uh-oh. Now that I feel good about the deal we just made, I don't want Felipe to call it off. What if the hovercraft has just stopped working? Will all of this be for nothing?

Wait a minute. Calm down, Billy. Check the fuel gauge.

Sure enough, the fuel tank is empty!

"Looks like we're out of fuel," I explain. "We're going to need another load of stinky socks."

Without missing a beat, as if powering a vehicle with stinky socks was something he did every day, Felipe pulls out a walkie-talkie and calls the studio's laundry department, where they wash the various costumes.

"I need stinky-type smelling socks," he says into the crackling device.

"I'm sorry, did you say smelling salts, Mr. LaVita?" asks the voice on the other end.

"No, no, darling, socks . . . socks that smell bad," Felipe says.

"Gotcha, Mr. LaVita," comes the reply. "Coming right up. You're in luck. We were just about to do a huge load of laundry."

As we wait for the laundry to arrive, Emily walks around the working hovercraft.

124

"Hmm," she says, nodding and looking at all of the hovercraft's parts. "Clever. I would not have thought of that."

"Greg was a big help," I say.

Just then, a golf cart pulling a trailer filled with a mountain of dirty socks pulls up. Everyone immediately pinches their noses closed and waves their hands in front of their faces to keep away the TERRIBLE SMELL.

"Why do stinky socks have to be so stinky?" asks Felipe.

I hop out of the hovercraft to help speed up the loading process. Manny and I shove the mound of socks into the fuel tank as fast as we can, securing the door tightly.

I climb back into the cockpit and push the starter button again. This time the hovercraft's engines roar to life. Pushing the controls forward, we lift off into the sky.

"Oooh, this is exciting!" squeals Felipe as we soar above the studio.

Felipe decides to give me his own personal tour.

"Down there, that is the costume shop," he begins, pointing to a long building.

I see people pushing racks of costumes out through the building's wide doors. On the racks hang everything from a knight's armor to a queen's ball gown, cowboy outfits with hats and boots, and a 1920s pinstripe suit, complete with shiny white shoes.

Felipe continues, "And that is the workshop where people build creatures and rockets and, ooh, look, a pirate ship!"

I glance down and see an authentic-looking pirate ship roll out of the workshop. It looks so real with its wooden decks, tall masts, and skull-and-crossbones flags all flapping in the wind.

The tour goes on, and I get so engrossed that I forget to keep track of the time—or the fuel gauge!

The hovercraft starts to sputter and lose altitude. I glance at the gauge. The arrow is practically touching the "E."

"So what is happening right now?" Felipe asks calmly, unaware of the imminent danger of crashing. "Is this BUMPY RIDE supposed to be so bumpy?"

"We're running out of fuel," I say as calmly as I can, trying to hide my own worry at the real possibility of a crash. There's only one thing to do. Not only do I need to pull off my own socks, but I have to ask this big-time Hollywood director to give me his.

"I hate to ask this of you, sir, but can I have your socks? We only need a few to give us the fuel we need to make a safe landing."

I start to pull off my own shoes and socks.

To my surprise and relief, Felipe does the same.

Gross!!! Felipe's socks have the STINKY SUPERPOWER of about a hundred other socks. They smell *really bad.*

"I always wear the same socks the ENTIRE

TIME I am making a movie," Felipe explains. "It is my superstition, but I am afraid that if I change my socks then the movie will be terrible. But in this case, here you go." He hands me the socks. I take them. I feel like I'm going to hurl.

Suddenly I feel really bad for the people who do Felipe's laundry.

"Thank you, Felipe," I say.

"It is nothing, my friend," Felipe replies.

"I have one more favor to ask of you," I say. "The fuel tank is down there on the side of the hovercraft. I need you to hold my ankles while I lean out and put the socks in."

"So what are we waiting for?" Felipe says. "Let's go!"

With Felipe holding my ankles, I lean out of the cockpit, grasping the socks in my hands.

"A little lower!" I shout back up.

Felipe leans down, moving me just close enough. I pop open the fuel tank, toss in the socks, then slam it closed.

"Okay! Pull me up!"

As Felipe pulls me back into the cockpit, I hear the engines pick up.

Tumbling into the pilot's seat, I guide the hovercraft back toward my family, landing safely on the ground.

"Thank you for helping," I say as we climb out. "I hope you weren't frightened."

"**NONSENSE!**" says Felipe, patting me on the back. "I trust you completely. But now it is time to make a movie!"

Felipe raises the megaphone to his lips.

"Oh, Frederick!" he shouts.

A few seconds later a young man appears. He is tall with short blond hair and carries a clipboard, a computer tablet, and a thick movie script. I glance at the script and see that it is for the movie that Manny, Emily, and I will be in—*Alien Zombie Attack!*

"Yes, Mr. LaVita?" says Frederick.

"Frederick, can you please take these nice people to makeup?" asks Felipe.

"You got it, Mr. LaVita," says Frederick. "Please come with me."

Manny and I climb into a golf cart, and Frederick drives us to the makeup department. On our phone call earlier, Greg said he wasn't interested in acting in the film as long as he got credited at the end. Felipe was happy to oblige.

In the makeup room, Manny and I sit in a tall chair, the kind you sit it for a haircut.

Two makeup artists appear and get to work.

"Hold very still, please," says the makeup artist. She paints jagged red streaks of dripping blood all around my mouth. "This will take about two minutes to dry."

I do my best to hold perfectly still for two minutes. Who knew that two minutes could feel like TWO HOURS!

Finally I am freed from my chair. I look over and gasp. Manny, who is getting out of the next chair, has been fully transformed into a totally creepy zombie.

"Whoa! You look amazing!"

"You too," says Manny. He points to a mirror on the wall behind me. I turn around and jump back in shock. It's a strange feeling to look at your own face in a mirror and see a zombie staring back, complete with rotted skin and dripping blood.

"Okay, boys, time to get you to the set," says Frederick, leading us back to his golf cart.

A couple minutes later we arrive at a remote corner of the lot. It is a thickly wooded area. Emily, still in her zombie makeup, is waiting for us. Dad is there too.

"So, Em, what do you think?" I say, making my scariest zombie face and GROWLING. Do zombies growl? I guess they make more of a moaning sound.

"What do I think about what?" she replies.

"About my zombie makeup?"

"Oh, I didn't notice. You look about THE SAME to me."

Movie star or not, she's still my big sister.

"You all look amazing!" Dad says, cracking up. "This is so cool!"

"All right, now!" Felipe shouts into his megaphone. "It is time to make a movie!"

Manny, Emily, and I follow Felipe and the camera crew into the woods. Waiting there are four teenage actors. They are not in zombie makeup. My guess is that they will end up being zombie dinner.

"Okay, everyone, listen up," Felipe announces into the megaphone. "In this scene, the teenagers are lost in the woods. They have made a wrong turn. Our lighting will make it look like the sun is about to set. And that is when the alien zombies show up."

Yup. I was right. ZOMBIE DINNER.

Frederick leads Manny, Emily, and me deep into the woods.

"When you hear the line, 'I guess we should have turned left, not right, at the big

rock,' that's when you attack," he explains. "Got it?"

"Got it," I say.

"Quiet now, everyone, please," Felipe shouts. "Roll the cameras . . . and ACTION!"

From our hiding place in the woods I see the four teenagers walking.

"I'm sure our campsite is *this* way," says a girl with red hair.

"We've been walking for an hour," says a short boy with dark brown hair and freckles, wearing a T-shirt that says: ZOMBIES? HA! BRING 'EM ON! "We should have passed the campsite a long time ago."

An owl hoots in the distance. Critters scamper through the fallen leaves. I feel myself getting scared—and I'm supposed to be the monster!

A second girl points in the direction from which the campers had just come.

"I guess we should have turned left, not right, at the big rock," she says.

That's it! WE'RE ON!

I stumble, stiff-legged from my hiding place.

"*Urrrrrgh!*" I moan, extending my arms as I lurch toward the teens. Manny and Emily do the same.

"Zombies!" screams the redheaded girl. "Run for your lives!"

As the teens run, Gemma Weston comes bursting through the bushes, confronting our little band of zombies.

"I'm Agent Jean, Zombie Division, and I'm here to save the day. Back off, zombies!" she cries, then pretends to suck us into her ZOM- BIE VACUUM!

"And . . . cut!" yells Felipe. "Wonderful! Beautiful! You are such naturals, I would think you are real alien zombies!"

We repeat the same scene as the camera moves to capture it from a few different angles. An hour later, our filming is all done.

"That was great fun!" I say as Frederick starts to remove the zombie makeup from my face.

Gemma comes over to me.

"I'm a huge fan of your company," she says. "Let me know if we can work together in the future. I'd love to be a celebrity spokesperson for Sure Things, Inc.! And, Em, stay in touch, okay?"

"Sure thing, Gem," replies Emily as Frederick removes her makeup and Gemma heads to her trailer.

"*Em?*" "*Gem?*" . . . Gee, Emily really did make friends with a real-life movie star. That is pretty cool.

"Thank you, Billy Sure, for your wonderful hovercraft," says Felipe, shaking my hand.

"You mean *your* Really Great Hovercraft, right?" I reply.

"You are right, Billy Sure. Good-bye to all of you. And thank you. Come visit anytime you like."

A short while later, Manny, Emily, Dad and I board a train headed for home, leaving the Really Great Hovercraft at the movie studio.

"So, WHAT'S NEXT?" Manny asks as we roll along the tracks.

"Well, Dad better teach me how to drive a car," Emily says, smiling.

"That's probably not going to happen for a while, since you're grounded for the rest of your life," says Dad. "And thankfully, I'm going to have help enforcing that grounding. I'M MAKING WAFFLES TONIGHT!"

I perk up. "Waffles? That means that Mom is coming home!"

Dad says nothing. He just smiles at me. Which is all the confirmation I need.

Meanwhile, Emily sniffles. "Grounded?" she says. "And more supervision. Just great. I wish I could be invisible."

Hmm. Invisibility.

Now that Sure Things, Inc. isn't working on the hovercraft—or selling it—we need a new Next Big Thing. Emily may not yet know it, but I think she just inspired a new idea. . . .

BILLY SURE
•KID ENTREPRENEUR•
AND THE
INVISIBLE
INVENTOR

PHILO

INVENTED BY LUKE SHARPE
DRAWINGS BY GRAHAM ROSS

Usually dinnertime at my house isn't something to look forward to. My dad likes to make all kinds of wacky dishes. My mom travels a lot for work. And my sister, Emily . . . let's just say she's not the nicest person in the world, all the time.

But tonight, dinner is different. That's because my family—and my best friend—are gathered around the kitchen table, eating the best take-out pizza in the whole wide world!

For those of you who may not have heard of me, my name is Billy Sure. I am one half of Sure Things, Inc., an invention company that I share with my best friend—and current pizza-eating pal—Manny Reyes.

About a week ago Manny, my dad, Emily, and I returned from an unplanned adventure at the Really Great Movies studio. Manny, Emily, and I got to play zombies in a new movie, Alien Zombie Attack! It's funny to think about it, because this all started when Emily stole my latest invention, a hovercraft, and crash-landed at the studio. We had to rescue her.

While at the movie studio, we sold the hovercraft—renamed the Really Great Hovercraft—to the film's director so he can use it in his films.

But Manny, being the super businessperson that he is, kept all the hovercraft's merchandising rights for Sure Things, Inc. That means money from any products related to the hovercraft get to stay ours. Pretty smart, huh? Because he sweats the fine print of every business deal is reason #934 why I'm glad that Manny is my best friend and business partner.

Although this happened a week ago, it still feels like just yesterday. On the actual "just yesterday," my mom came back from her latest work trip. I say "work trip," but it's much cooler than that—my mom is a spy. She's away on different missions a lot.

For her current mission Mom is able to work remotely from home. I really miss her when she's not around, so it's great having her here, for lots of reasons. One of those reasons is that, unlike my dad, Mom loves to order in food—like this super-awesome twelve-cheese pizza!

"I didn't even know there were twelve different kinds of cheeses," Mom says, biting into her slice.

Dad munches happily, pausing every so often to smile and say "yum!" These days, Dad seems to have a permanent smile on his face. And for good reason.

"I can't believe my art show is just a few days away," Dad says through a mouthful of cheese. "But I wonder if I need another painting of Philo's paw...."

Oh yeah, I forgot to tell you. Dad may be a terrible cook, but he's a terrific artist. I think. I guess I don't know much about art. His latest series of paintings is going to be displayed at a gallery. They are mostly paintings of my dog Philo's tongue, Philo's paws, and oddly enough, Philo's butt.

Dad also has a few paintings of some of the food he's made, like tomato pancakes and cherry-and-kiwi lasagna. The paintings may just be tastier than the food itself—though I've never taken a bite out of one.

I've finished my first slice of pizza when I hear Manny's voice.

"Ready for another one?" he asks from across the table.

"Thanks, partner, but I can get it myself," I reply. "You don't have to get up."

"Who said anything about getting up?"

Manny pulls out his smartphone and taps the screen. From across the room, a slice of pizza comes flying through the air, right at me!

"Manny!" I cry. "Did you invent flying pizza?!"

Before Manny can answer, I snatch the slice out of the air. There, hanging in the air, is a small, perfectly accurate model of the Really Great Hovercraft! The pizza had been resting on the model.

"I didn't invent flying pizza, but I did come up with a remote-controlled model of the hovercraft," Manny explains. "I control it right from my smartphone."

Manny swipes his phone, and the tiny hover-craft turns around and speeds back to the pizza boxes on the counter.

"Awesome," I say. "I think this toy is going to be a huge hit!"

"I'd like some flying pizza too," says Mom.

"Sure," Manny says.

With Manny tapping and swiping his phone, the tiny hovercraft slides under another slice, turns around, speeds back through the air, and deposits a slice of pizza onto Mom's plate.

BAM! That's when the front door bursts open. You might have noticed that my sister Emily has been absent from dinner so far. (Okay, I kind of forgot too.) That's because she was walking Philo, who scurries in, pulling hard on his leash.

"Easy, Philo!" Emily says. "Slow down!"

Are you surprised that Emily is the one walking Philo, and not me? Well, you should be. Before we returned from our trip to the Really Great Movies studio, I could count on two hands the number of times that Emily had volunteered to walk Philo.

Uh, now that I think about it . . . make that one hand.

But as punishment for stealing my hover-craft, Dad grounded Emily for life. He was probably exaggerating about the lifelong sentence part, though, because he made a deal with her. If Emily is as nice and helpful as she possibly can be, and does one nice big thing for everyone in the family, she will be ungrounded.

Well, since making that deal, it's like Emily is a whole new person. She takes out the garbage, cleans the dinner dishes, and volunteers to walk Philo every evening! I've been calling her Super Nice Emily. I know she hates the nickname, but she has to be nice and can't say anything about it.

I could get used to this!

"I wish Philo wouldn't pull on his leash when I take him for a walk," Emily says.

Before I have a chance to explain that all

she has to do is say "heel" and he'll walk nicely beside you, Philo spots the flying hovercraft toy zooming through the air.

Philo starts barking wildly at the hovercraft and takes off after it, dragging Emily through the kitchen and back into the living room. I have to admit, it's really funny. Emily jumps over a chair, then stumbles to avoid crashing into a table.

The hovercraft turns back toward the kitchen. Philo suddenly changes direction to keep up with it, causing Emily to knock a lamp from a table.

She spins back and catches the lamp just before it hits the floor.

This is really entertaining to watch. I consider letting it go on a little longer, but, well, that would just be mean.

"Let go of the leash, Emily!" I shout, cracking up.

She lets go. Philo continues to chase the hovercraft until Manny guides it back into his hands.

Emily joins us, trying to catch her breath. Her curly hair has flopped into her face. Her shirt has come untucked. She's a mess, which normally would make her very upset and require extensive repair time in front of a mirror. But Super Nice Emily doesn't say complain.

"Well, I walked Philo again," she says, forcing a smile.

"We know, dear," says Mom. "Why don't you join us and have some pizza?"

"I will," says Emily. "But first everyone has to come outside and see the great job I did washing the car! And since everyone rides in the car, it's something nice I did for the whole family."

"You washed the car?" I ask in disbelief. Even for Super Nice Emily, this is above and beyond. "Now, this I have to see!"

We all get up and hurry outside.

"Well, what do you think?" asks Emily.

I look over at the car and see that it is covered in soap. Bubbly white streaks drip down the doors and windows.

"Maybe Dad can paint a picture of this for his art show," I say. Usually, I go out of my way not to give Emily a hard time. The grief I always get from her in return is just not worth the fun. But with her having to be nice and helpful to everybody, I figure I've got a free pass. "Dad can call the painting Half-Washed Car."

"I appreciate the effort, Emily," says Mom, raising her eyebrows slightly at me. "But you have to rinse the soap off."

A few minutes later everyone except Emily is back inside, and Manny is really getting into delivering pizza slices using the hover-craft toy.

"I'll take another one, Manny." says Dad. "I'm curious how they can stuff the cheese inside the cheese."

Manny taps and swipes his phone, tilting it a bit left, then right. The hovercraft toy scoops up a slice of pizza, circles the living room, then comes back into the kitchen, dropping gently down until it stops, hovering in midair right above Dad's plate.

"Thanks, Manny," says Dad, taking the slice. He stares at the cheese-stuffed cheese. "Hmm . . . so that's how they do it."

Emily comes back inside. "Well, the car is clean," she says. "All the soap is off."

And I can see where it went. Emily's clothes are now streaked with white bubbly soapsuds! She looks wet from head to toe. I almost feel bad for her. It's probably not nice to be enjoying this as much as I am, but I am!

"You should change into some warm clothes," says Mom. "Then come have a slice of pizza."

When Emily finally sits down, Manny delivers her a slice with the hovercraft.

"Thank you, Manny," she says, digging into her pizza. "And congratulations on your new toy. Another Sure Things, Inc. success!"

After every slice has been devoured Emily is the first one to jump up from the table. "Here," she says. "Let me get those for everyone."

She goes around the table, picking up all

the plates and cups. Then she washes, dries, and puts away each one.

"There, everything's clean," she says as a glob of soapsuds (this time, from the kitchen) drops from her shirt onto her shoes.

Ding dong!

The doorbell. Hmm, we're not expecting anyone. Out of habit, I start toward the door.

"Oh, no, Billy," Emily says sweetly. "Let me answer the door."

I better enjoy this while I can, because I have a feeling that once Emily gets out of her grounded-for-life sentence, she's gonna make me pay for all her niceness—big time!

Emily opens the front door.

"Hi, is Billy home?" asks a woman at the door. "I'd love to conduct an interview with him this evening."

I immediately feel a knot forming in my stomach. I know that voice. It's Kathy Jenkins. She's a reporter for Right Next Door, our local hometown news website. She's also Samantha's mother. Samantha is a member of my inventor's club, but she also helped me come up with the hovercraft design and used to follow me around the halls at school.

Kathy has written articles before about Sure Things, Inc. She always focuses on me, leaving out Manny's role in the company. And she can be nasty. She even wrote one time that Philo smells like a skunk.

What could she possibly want now?

I walk over to greet Kathy.

As much as I would love to, I can't refuse to talk with the press. That wouldn't do anything good for Sure Things, Inc. And I know Manny wouldn't want that.

"How are you, Billy?" Kathy says, extending her hand.

I shake her hand. Then we both take seats in the living room.

She glances into the kitchen, where Manny is teaching Dad how to pilot the hovercraft toy. She seems unfazed!

"So," Kathy says, pressing play on her portable recorder. "Tell me about Danny."

"Danny?" I ask. "Who's Danny?"

She raises her eyebrows as if to say, Why are you trying to make this difficult?

"Danny. Your partner," she repeats.

"Manny," I correct her. "His name is Manny."

I'm glad she's finally interested in Manny, but can't she get his name right?

"Yes, Manny, of course. Tell me about Manny."

Finally a chance to set the record straight.

"Well, basically, without Manny, there is no Sure Things, Inc.," I begin. "Everything we do, we do as a team. We work really well together and make every important decision as partners. The nicest part is that through it all we've been able to stay best friends. And really, I think that's why we work so well together, and why Sure Things, Inc. has been successful."

"So do you do all the inventing, and Danny handles all the business and marketing?" asks Kathy.

"Manny," I correct her. Again. "And for the

most part that's true, but take a look at this."

I quickly download the app Manny created onto my phone. Then I tap the screen. The hovercraft toy comes flying into the living room. I swipe the screen and the toy circles the room once, then comes in for a soft landing right at my feet.

"This is the Really Great Hovercraft Toy," I explain. "This was all Manny's idea. He wrote the app and built a replica of our hovercraft—only mini!"

"But I thought that Sure Things, Inc. sold the rights of the hovercraft to Really Great Movies?" says Kathy.

This is perfect. She just set me up to show how smart Manny really is.

"Well, actually, we did," I explain. "The movie studio is using the hovercraft in their movies and theme parks. But, because Manny is such a good businessperson, we kept all the merchandising rights."

I tap my phone again, and the hovercraft toy lifts up and zooms back into the kitchen.

"I just love this," Kathy squeals. "Who knew that Danny was the hidden face of Sure Things, Inc.?"

"Manny," I say, "and it's really no secret. Manny has been there from the start. He's always been a huge and equal part of the company. You know, I have tried to tell you this before. And I have tried to bring Manny in on some of our earlier interviews. But you always seem to—"

"Tell me this, Billy," Kathy interrupts me. It's clear she doesn't want to listen. "Who really came up with the name Disappearing Reappearing Makeup?"

"That was Manny."

"The Gross-to-Good Powder?"

"That was Manny too."

"Fascinating," says Kathy.

I should be happy that she's looking to give Manny credit, but I feel uneasy. I just don't trust her. Even now.

"So, it appears that Danny is extremely important to Sure Things, Inc.," Kathy says.

Why won't she use his real name?

"His name is Manny, and yes, that's what I've been trying to tell you since our very first interview."

Kathy stands up suddenly. I get up too.

"This was great, Billy," she says, shaking my hand. "Thank you for your time, and be sure to read Right Next Door tomorrow! We'll be happy to tell everyone about Manny."

"Danny," I hiss, and then I take it back. Oh no! Did Kathy use his correct name to trip me up?

Without saying anything, Kathy hurries to the front door and leaves just as quickly as she arrived.

I rejoin the others in the kitchen.

"I can't believe her!" I say, grabbing my head with both hands.

"What happened?" asks Mom.

I fill everyone in on the interview—including my flub at the end. Then I look right at Manny, who's been busy checking company e-mail on his phone.

"She finally wants to include your contributions and she can't even bother to get your name right!"

Manny just shakes his head and smiles.

"She can call me Franny for all I care," Manny says. "In fact, she can call me anything she likes, as long as she mentions Sure Things, Inc. and the Really Great Hovercraft Toy. We get publicity. We move merchandise. It's all good, Billy!"

Well, I suppose he's right, as usual.